THE MAN WHO TAMED MALLORY

Brad Gourlay and his ruthless band of gunslingers ruled the small mining town of Mallory, and the townsfolk lived in continual fear for their lives. Then, by chance, the Governor of Colorado was visited by an old comrade-in-arms, the Kentuckian gunfighter, Jack Stone, whom he asked to mount an undercover investigation. And, when Stone rode into Mallory, Gourlay and his gang quickly discovered that they were up against one of the deadliest and most dangerous men in the West.

Books by J. D. Kincaid
in the Linford Western Library:

CORRIGAN'S REVENGE
THE FOURTH OF JULY
SHOWDOWN AT MEDICINE CREEK
COYOTE WINTER
JUDGEMENT AT RED ROCK

J. D. KINCAID

THE MAN WHO TAMED MALLORY

Complete and Unabridged

LINFORD
Leicester

First published in Great Britain in 1994 by
Robert Hale Limited
London

First Linford Edition
published 1996
by arrangement with
Robert Hale Limited
London

British Library CIP Data

Kincaid, J. D.
  The man who tamed Mallory.—Large print ed.—
Linford western library
I. Title II. Series
823.914 [F]

ISBN 0–7089–7814–2

Published by
F. A. Thorpe (Publishing) Ltd.
Anstey, Leicestershire

Set by Words & Graphics Ltd.
Anstey, Leicestershire
Printed and bound in Great Britain by
T. J. Press (Padstow) Ltd., Padstow, Cornwall

This book is printed on acid-free paper

Author's Note

In various of my 'Jack Stone' novels, mention has been made of the fact that Stone was the man who tamed Mallory, the roughest, toughest town in all Colorado. This, then, is the story of how Stone succeeded in bringing law and order to that notorious hell-hole and, in doing so, became a legend of the West.

To Rita and Frank

1

BRAD GOURLAY held the small mining town of Mallory in the palm of his hand. It had once been a sleepy one-horse town, the heart of a peaceful farming community. Then, with the discovery of gold in the territory, all hell had broken loose and now Mallory was a devil's crucible, a place where the original inhabitants lived in continual fear of their lives. Not only prospectors and miners, but outlaws, gamblers and all manner of riff-raff, provided they had money in their pockets, had been encouraged by Brad Gourlay to cross the state line into Colorado, and stop over in Mallory and spend their ill-gotten dollars in its saloons and bordellos.

Originally, there had been but one saloon and no bordellos. Now there were three saloons and seven bordellos.

Brad Gourlay owned two of the former and four of the latter. He also owned Mallory's one and only hotel, its livery stables, two of its five stores and the Mallory Mining Company.

Law and order, such as it was, was supposedly administered by Sheriff Joe Banks, a fat toad of a man who did exactly what Brad Gourlay told him to do. In fact, Gourlay's hired guns under their leader, Long Tom Russell, made sure that no damage was done to any of his establishments, or, if it was, that generous recompense was made. They also made sure that those establishments which Gourlay did not own paid tribute to him. At first there had been protests against this, but, after Long Tom and his gang had gunned down a couple of complaining storekeepers, the protests had ceased and the others paid up promptly, if unwillingly.

Consequently, Brad Gourlay had soon become a very rich man indeed and, with a judicious mixture of bribery and coercion, had eventually got himself elected mayor. However, this was not enough.

While his mining company was working the main seam located in the hills outside Mallory, there was also a large number of other seams being worked by other prospectors. To save them the trouble of journeying to the state capital, Denver, to register their claims, the Office of Land Registry had opened a branch office in Mallory. This was managed by a small, bespectacled clerk named Norman Lowery, a man who, Brad Gourlay quickly discovered, was open to corruption.

Gourlay's scheme was a simple one. He ordered Long Tom Russell and his men to keep their eyes open for any prospector who had come into Mallory for provisions. Then, one of the gang would engage the prospector in conversation, maybe buy him a few drinks, and attempt to find out whether or not he had struck it rich.

If he had, Long Tom would arrange to have the prospector bushwhacked on his way back to his claim, and Brad Gourlay would then get Norman Lowery to alter his records to show the claim as registered to his, Gourlay's Mallory Mining Company. In this way, the Mallory Mining Company acquired one after another of the best strikes in and around Mallory.

This was the situation when, on one wet and windy October afternoon, Brad Gourlay had an unexpected visitor.

He was comfortably ensconced in one of the upstairs bedrooms of the Ace High Saloon. This was probably the most lucrative of Mallory's three saloons and was, of course, owned by Gourlay. Its management, however, he left in the capable hands of Nancy Carson, a thirty-year-old blonde who, in her time, had been an actress, a saloon girl, a croupier, a partner in an ill-fated perfume business and housekeeper to a preacher who had absconded with the church funds. In

4

fact, a woman of vast and varied experience.

Nancy, although now rather plump, remained a warm, attractive woman, and she had foolishly fallen head over heels in love with Brad Gourlay. He, for his part, was attracted to Nancy and happy enough to bed her. But he had no plans to marry her, for his ambitions did not begin and end at Mallory. When he had accumulated sufficient money, he intended to move on, perhaps go East and set himself up in some respectable business like real estate. Then he might enter politics, maybe stand for Congress or the Senate. And, if he did, he would need a wife who would be an asset to him. Nancy Carson would not do at all.

The rain was beating furiously against the window panes on that wild October afternoon, and Brad Gourlay was relaxing in bed with a glass of whiskey and a large cigar, while Nancy cuddled up beside him. They had enjoyed their usual strenuous bout of lovemaking and, in its aftermath, Gourlay lounged back on the pillows and quietly sipped his whiskey and puffed on his cigar.

"Mmm, this is nice, Brad," murmured Nancy drowsily.

"It sure is. A li'l peace 'n' quiet is jest what . . . "

But Brad Gourlay never finished that sentence, for he was interrupted by the bedroom door suddenly flying open and Pete Norris, one of Long Tom Russell's gunslingers, erupting into the room.

"What in tarnation d'you think yo're doin', Pete?" yelled Brad Gourlay angrily.

"S . . . sorry, Mr Gourlay, but this here feller stuck a gun in my ribs an' forced me to take him to you," gasped Norris.

Brad Gourlay looked round at the man who had followed Pete Norris into the room. His eyes widened in surprise and he let loose a bellow of laughter.

"Goddammit, Nate, when did you blow into town?" he demanded.

The stranger grinned.

"'Bout five minutes ago, I guess," he drawled.

"Wa'al I'll be darned!"

Brad Gourlay leapt from the bed and, although completely naked, went over and embraced the newcomer without the slightest hesitation or embarrassment. Nancy Carson was rather less uninhibited. She hastily pulled up the bedclothes to cover her breasts. She might have known many men in her lifetime, but, when she entertained them in her bedroom, it was invariably one at a time. Pete Norris was equally flabbergasted. He stood staring at the two men, with his eyes popping and his jaw hanging open.

Eventually, the pair broke from their embrace and Brad Gourlay turned to the others.

"This here's my brother, Nathan," he explained. "We ain't seen each other in 'bout four years."

"That's right, Brad," said Nathan Gourlay. "We last met down in

7

Phoenix, at Ma's funeral. You had jest set up in business here, an' you invited me to come 'n' join you."

"So I did. But you reckoned you had other fish to fry."

"Yeah. Wa'al, things didn't work out an', in the end, I had to lam outta Arizona in one helluva hurry."

"Is that a fact?"

"I'll tell you 'bout it later," said Nathan, directing a quick glance at the other two in the room.

Brad Gourlay nodded.

"Sure thing, Nate. Whenever yo're ready," he said.

"Yeah. Wa'al, for now, reckon what I need is some good ole red-eye followed by a nice juicy steak. Then, afterwards, mebbe I'll have me a good hot bath an' a nice, juicy woman."

"Like Nancy here?"

"Exactly like Nancy." Nathan Gourlay grinned at the blonde. "Pleased to meet you, ma'am," he said politely.

"Pleased to meet you, Nate," replied Nancy, although, in fact, she did not like the lustful glint in his eye.

She regarded the two brothers with a steady stare. There could be no mistaking the relationship. The same dark hair, beetling eyebrows, high cheekbones, large nose and square jaw proclaimed them as brothers. But Brad was the sturdier and slightly taller of the two. Nathan's face and figure were lean and bony, and he had a hungry-looking air about him. Also, his eyes, unlike his brother's, were slate-grey and as cold as the winter wind. Nancy guessed that, despite his initial politeness, Nathan Gourlay would prove to be a demanding and sadistic bedfellow.

Brad Gourlay dismissed Pete Norris and, thereupon, quickly dressed. He donned an expensive white shirt with a ruffled collar, a black string tie, and an immaculately-cut dark grey city-style suit. And, beneath the jacket, he wore a bright crimson velvet vest, this last item of clothing adding a touch of flamboyance to his otherwise rather conservative appearance. Finally, he placed his gold hunter in his vest pocket and strapped on his gun-belt. He carried a forty-five calibre, pearl-handled British Tranter tied down on his right thigh.

Nathan Gourlay was much less expensively attired in a badly faded red and white check shirt, black leather vest and levis, all worn beneath an ancient ankle-length leather coat. But he was as well-armed as his brother, carrying a Remington revolver and, in a sheath at his waist, a Bowie knife.

As the two brothers left the bedchamber and headed downstairs to the bar-room, Brad Gourlay turned and addressed the blonde.

"Git yoreself outta that bed, Nancy, an' come down an' join us," he said.

"Okay. I'll be down directly," replied Nancy.

She rose and proceeded to dress herself in a dark red, low-cut velvet gown. Then, she set about powdering her face and tidying her hair. Nancy took a fierce pride in her appearance and had no intention of leaving the bedroom until she was satisfied that she was looking her best.

By the time Nancy entered the saloon, the brothers were onto their third whiskey and had been joined at the bar by Brad Gourlay's right-hand man, the gunslinger, Long Tom Russell.

Long Tom made the Gourlays, neither of whom was under six feet, look positively short. A bean-pole of a man, he stood six foot six inches in his stockinged feet and was dressed entirely in black, from his low-crowned Stetson to his unspurred boots. And he wore two guns, a pair of well-used Colt Peacemakers. Long black hair hung down beneath the brim of his Stetson and cruel black eyes stared out of the man's thin, wolfish face. He fingered his pencil-thin moustache and leered at the blonde.

"Howdy, boys," said Nancy and, smiling at Brad Gourlay, she added, "I'll have my usual."

11

"A tequila for Miss Nancy," said Brad Gourlay.

"Thanks. You enjoyin' yoreself, Nate?" asked Nancy.

"Sure am. It's been a long, wet ride to Mallory, an' I can tell you it sure feels good to be in the dry."

"Yeah, I can imagine. It don't seem to have stopped rainin' for 'bout a week or more."

"Nope." Nathan Gourlay slapped his belly. "An' now I reckon I could do justice to a nice, big steak," he declared hungrily.

Brad Gourlay glanced across at Nancy.

"Best steaks in town are served at the Grand Hotel," he stated.

"Reckon yo're sayin' that 'cause you own that there hotel," said Nathan perceptively.

His brother grinned.

"I own most of Mallory. An' what I don't own, I claim tribute from. Believe me, Nate, I got this town all stitched up."

"I believe you, Brad. Now, 'bout that steak . . . "

"Oh, yeah. 'Course." Brad Gourlay again glanced across at Nancy. "Go fetch Nate a steak, will yuh?" he asked.

"But, Brad, it's pourin' with rain out there!" demurred Nancy.

"So, the hotel's only next door an' you got an umbrella, ain't yuh?"

"Yes, but . . . "

"Go git Nate a steak, an' be darned quick about it," snapped Brad Gourlay.

Nancy paled beneath her powder. Usually, she could handle the town mayor. However, she knew better than to cross him.

"Okay, Brad, I'll . . . I'll do that," she stammered.

Nancy could not find an umbrella, so she had to make do with a parasol. Clutching this, she hurried across the saloon towards the batwing doors. As she reached them, two men burst in and pushed past her without a word. Nancy's curiosity was roused.

Normally, both Sheriff Joe Banks and the Land Registry clerk, Norman Lowery, would have stopped and greeted her. So, what the hell was the matter? Both had looked decidedly grim-faced. Nancy shrugged her plump white shoulders. Doubtless, in due course, she would find out what was happening. For the present, she had to do Brad Gourlay's bidding. Therefore, putting up her parasol, Nancy pushed open the batwing doors and plunged out into the rain.

Sheriff Joe Banks and Norman Lowery made an incongruous pair, the former fat and bloated in his huge sheepskin coat, and the latter a tiny rat of a man in a shiny brown city-style suit. Banks' puffy red face and Lowery's pinched, pale features behind steel-framed spectacles both bore expressions of unmitigated gloom.

Brad Gourlay leant across the hammered copper bar-top and ordered a couple of whiskies for the sheriff and the Land Registry clerk. Then he turned and said, "Okay, boys, why are you two lookin' like the end of the world is nigh?"

"'Cause we're in big trouble, that's why!" exclaimed Joe Banks.

"What kinda trouble?" demanded Brad Gourlay.

"There's gonna be an investigation," said Norman Lowery.

"An investigation! What kinda investigation?"

"An investigation into the runnin' of the Land Registry office," said the sheriff.

"That's right. My superiors are sendin' someone along to check up on my records here in Mallory," said Lowery.

"From yore headquarters in Denver?"

"Yes, Mr Gourlay."

"Who are they sendin'? Do you know?"

"Yeah. A young feller named Benjamin Dexter."

"So, mebbe we can persuade him to

okay yore records?"

"Not Dexter."

"No?"

"No. I know the man. He's totally incorruptible."

"Wa'al, mebbe he won't find nuthin'."

"Are you kiddin', Mr Gourlay?"

"No, I ain't kiddin'. Yo're supposed to have doctored yore records so as they look all straight 'n' above board."

"They do."

"Wa'al, then?"

"A cursory examination wouldn't reveal a thing. But this is gonna be a rigorous, in-depth investigation. An' believe me, Mr Gourlay, Benjamin Dexter is one smart sonofabitch. He'll sure as hell find somethin'."

"Aw, goddammit!"

Nathan Gourlay looked curiously at his brother and asked, "What's this all about, Brad?"

"We've been jumpin' a few claims."

"Whaddya mean?"

"Long Tom an' his boys have rubbed out a few prospectors who have struck it rich. An' Mr Lowery here has altered his records to show their claims as registered in the name of the Mallory Mining Company, my company."

"I see."

"It seemed foolproof. Prospectors are, by an' large, loners. Who was gonna miss a few of 'em?"

"Somebody did, it appears."

"Yeah. My guess is that some of their fellow-prospectors have smelt a rat," said Sheriff Joe Banks. "It only takes one or two to talk an' then a rumour spreads."

"As far as Denver?" said Brad Gourlay.

"It looks like it," said the sheriff.

"So, what are you gonna do?" asked Nathan.

"Dunno," said his brother morosely.

"Let me handle this for you, boss," said Long Tom Russell, fingering the butts of his Colt Peacemakers.

"Hell, no!" exclaimed Brad Gourlay. "You gun down this Benjamin Dexter an', the next thing you know, the

Governor will send in a posse of US marshals to find out what's goin' on here."

"Mr Gourlay's right," declared Joe Banks. "We don't wanta do nuthin' to prompt the Governor into orderin' a full-scale investigation. Then we'd really be in trouble!"

"So, what in tarnation do we do?" demanded Long Tom Russell.

"Like I already said, I dunno," said Brad Gourlay. "You'll have to let me think on it. Reckon I'll come up with somethin'."

"Wa'al, you ain't got long, Mr Gourlay," remarked Lowery anxiously. "The telegraph I received said Dexter'd be arrivin' in Mallory on tomorrow's noon-day stage."

Brad Gourlay nodded. He was not a man to show much emotion, but he was as worried as hell. Mallory was his. He had not spent the last four years attaining his present position in the town, just to have some two-bit government clerk destroy it with

18

a damning report to the Office of Land Registry in Denver. He would think of something. He must think of something. In the meantime, he ordered another round of whiskies.

It was while they were sipping their red-eye that Nathan Gourlay intervened. A thin smile played upon his lips and a malevolent gleam lighted up his cold, slate-grey eyes.

"I think I can take care of this feller, Dexter," he drawled.

"Without precipitatin' a visit from the US marshals' office in Denver?" enquired his brother.

"I guess that can be avoided," said Nathan.

"But how?"

"We let him complete his investigation an' head back on the stage for Denver."

"But that's crazy! If 'n' we do that, he'll file his report an' . . . " began Norman Lowery.

"No, he won't," said Nathan. "Y'see, I'll be travellin' with him, an' I'll see to it that his report shows nuthin' is amiss, that everythin' is fair an' square."

"I don't see how."

"Is Dexter a married man?"

"Yeah."

"Has he any children?"

"A coupla kids. A boy an' a girl."

Nathan Gourlay grinned wolfishly.

"Then, yore worries are over. Jest leave everythin' to me," he said. "I'll engage him in conversation 'fore he leaves Mallory an' then . . . "

"S'pose he don't wanta talk to you?" interjected Brad.

"Oh, I'm sure he'll be quite happy to talk to a US marshal."

"But you ain't no marshal."

"Nope, but I've got me a US marshal's badge."

Nathan Gourlay smiled and produced the badge from his vest pocket. He tossed it onto the hammered copper bar-counter. Eagerly, his brother picked it up and examined it. Brad Gourlay whistled softly.

"Hell, this is the real McCoy!" he exclaimed.

"Taken off a real-life marshal, who is now a real-dead marshal," explained Nathan, with a crooked grin.

"Ah, so that's why you had to lam outta Arizona in a hurry!" cried Brad Gourlay.

"Yup."

"So, let's assume you do manage to engage Dexter in conversation, what's yore plan, Nate?"

"That's for yore ears only," said Nathan and, turning to the others, he remarked quietly, "No offence, fellers, but I reckon the fewer folk who are privy to my li'l scheme, the better."

"Fair enough," said Long Tom Russell.

"Yeah. As the law around here, I don't wanta know," added Sheriff Joe Banks.

"Nor me," muttered Norman Lowery. He was already beginning to regret his unholy alliance with Brad Gourlay, and he had no wish to be implicated in the murder of his colleague. Not that Nathan Gourlay had spoken of killing

Benjamin Dexter. Still, Lowery had a nasty feeling that that was exactly what he intended.

Brad Gourlay had no such qualms about his brother murdering Dexter. Providing it did not rebound upon him, he was quite happy that Nathan should kill the investigator.

"To Nate's success!" he said, raising his glass and despatching the whiskey in one gulp.

As he did so, the batwing doors flew open and Nancy Carson dashed into the saloon. She held her parasol in one hand and, in the other, a large white plate, on which lay a T-bone steak so big that it hung over the edge.

"Ah, now that's what I call a steak!" cried Nathan Gourlay, licking his lips and eyeing the T-bone hungrily.

2

IT was as Benjamin Dexter was having a meal, prior to leaving Mallory on the noon-day stage, that he was approached by Nathan Gourlay. He was sitting in the dining-room of the Grand Hotel when he suddenly became aware of a figure standing over him. He glanced up and saw a tall, lean man, smartly rigged out in a black Derby hat, white shirt, black string tie, knee-length black jacket, grey velvet vest, black trousers and black leather, unspurred boots. Nathan had, for the moment, discarded his Bowie knife, though he continued to carry the Remington in his holster, and he looked every inch the lawman he was about to portray.

"Mind if I join you?" enquired Nathan Gourlay.

"Er . . . no . . . no. Do please sit

down," replied Dexter politely.

"Thanks." The gunslinger sat down and ordered a coffee. Then he remarked quietly, "Wa'al, I'll sure be glad to shake the dust of Mallory off my feet."

"Me, too," sighed Benjamin Dexter. "The law in this hell-hole ain't worth a red cent."

"You can say that again! I reckon it needs a whole posse of US marshals to ride in an' clean it up."

"Mebbe that's what it'll git."

"Howdya mean?"

Nathan Gourlay smiled and flicked open his jacket to reveal, pinned to the outside of his vest pocket, the US marshal's badge he had stolen from its late owner.

"Jeeze, are you a marshal?" exclaimed Dexter.

"Yup. Marshal John Smith at yore service," said Nathan, and he extended his hand towards the Land Registry clerk.

Benjamin Dexter took the proffered hand and introduced himself in turn.

"Benjamin Dexter, though you can call me Ben. I'm an employee of the Office of Land Registry."

"Really?

"Yeah. I've been visitin' our branch office in Mallory. An' you, Marshal, what are you doin' in Mallory?"

"I'm under cover, jest lookin' around. Gotta report back to the US Marshals' Office in Denver."

"Oh, yeah? An' can you tell me what yo're gonna report?" asked Dexter curiously.

"Wa'al, I shouldn't."

"But I'm a government employee like yoreself. You can trust me."

"I s'pose I can," Nathan rubbed his jaw and then, lowering his voice, murmured confidingly, "There ain't much to tell. The town's wide open, as you know. All kinds of riff-raff are holed up here. There's shootin's, an' stabbin's, an' drunken brawls, an' damage to property galore. But that's the sheriff's business. I cain't tell him how to do his job. He's been duly elected, as has Brad Gourlay, the mayor, the man who runs Mallory and who has the sheriff in his pocket."

"Yeah. Wa'al, my guess is, those elections were rigged."

"Yo're probably right, Ben. But how do you prove it?"

"I dunno."

"That's the rub. I know Brad Gourlay is corrupt. I know Sheriff Joe Banks is corrupt. However, without proof . . ."

"I thought you said that a posse of US marshals was gonna ride in an' . . ."

"I said mebbe they would. That's certainly what I'm gonna recommend, though, since I ain't got no actual proof against either Gourlay or the sheriff, the Governor may not be prepared to authorise such a move."

"There must be some decent citizens in Mallory, the ones who were here before Brad Gourlay turned it into the hell-hole it is now. Surely, you can persuade one or two of them to testify against Gourlay? They must, between them, have sufficient evidence for you to present to the Governor."

Nathan Gourlay smiled grimly.

"I'm afraid they're all too darned scared to speak out," he said.

"I see." Benjamin Dexter smiled a smug smile and whispered, "My business in Mallory has also been in the form of an enquiry. An' I believe I can give you the evidence you need to mount a full-scale official investigation."

"Is that a fact?" Nathan Gourlay bent forward and fixed the young clerk with an eager, anxious eye.

"Yes, Marshal, it is." Benjamin Dexter glanced round to make fully sure he was not likely to be overheard, and then he proceeded to tell Nathan Gourlay of how rumours had reached Denver regarding the disappearance of several gold prospectors from their claims and of the subsequent working of those claims by employees of Brad Gourlay's Mallory Mining Company.

27

"Consequently," he said, "I was despatched to Mallory to check the records at our Land Registry office here, to discover whether there had been any collusion between our clerk, Norman Lowery, and the Mallory Mining Company."

"And had there been?"

"Oh yes! Norman Lowery had done a good job in falsifying the records. They would have passed any routine check. But, of course, I knew what I was looking for."

"So, Brad Gourlay's goose is well an' truly cooked, huh?"

"That's right, Marshal. When I present my report to my boss, he will be sure to take the matter to the Governor, and then your office will undoubtedly be asked to investigate."

"Fine! That's jest dandy! Reckon it must be one helluva damnin' report?"

"Oh, it is!"

"Have you actually written it yet?"

"Yes, it's in my valise. I plan to hand it over to my boss, Mr Logan, first thing in the mornin', the day after we hit town."

"The stage is due in tomorrow 'bout mid-afternoon, right?"

"Right."

"Then, why the delay?"

"Tomorrow's Thursday an' every Thursday afternoon Mr Logan has a meetin' with the Governor an' various other heads of department." Dexter smiled cheerfully and continued, "Don't reckon a few hours' delay will matter much an', 'sides, I'm anxious to git home."

"A family man, huh?"

"Yup. Got me the finest li'l wife in all Colorado, an' two swell kids. Cain't wait to see 'em all again."

"You live in Denver, Ben?"

"I do. I have a nice, white-painted frame house in Silver Street, 'bout fifteen minutes' walk from my office."

"That's convenient."

"Sure is."

"You sound like a mighty contented man, Ben."

"I am."

"An' so you should be. Nice wife. Nice kids. It would be a pity if anythin' happened to 'em."

Benjamin Dexter froze. The menace in Nathan Gourlay's voice was unmistakable. He turned to stare at the fake marshal and found himself gazing into the other's pitiless, slate-grey eyes. All at once, he understood.

"You . . . you ain't no marshal!" he gasped.

"Nope."

"But that badge?"

"It's genuine. Its previous owner is kickin' up daisies."

"No!"

"Yeah."

"Then, who . . . who are you?"

"The name's Nathan Gourlay. I'm Brad Gourlay's younger brother."

"Oh, my God!"

"Scared, Ben?"

"Look, you can do what you like to me, but you leave my family alone!"

"That depends 'pon you, Ben."

"Upon me? What the hell do you mean?"

"That report. It jest won't do."

"Now, see here . . . "

"No, you see here. The report yo're gonna submit to yore Mr Logan is gonna state quite categorically that Norman Lowery's records are in order, an' all claims registered by the Mallory Minin' company are legitimate. Is that clear?"

Dexter continued to stare into the other's eyes, and what he saw scared him rigid. They were the eyes of an utterly ruthless, cold-blooded killer.

"An' if . . . if I refuse to alter my report?" he asked, white-faced.

"Yore wife an' kids will meet with a nasty accident."

"You . . . you'd never git away with . . . with . . . "

"With what, Ben? That's the point. You don't know what I plan doin', or how I plan doin' it, or even if I intend carryin' it out myself. Believe me, yore family are doomed should you refuse

31

me this li'l favour."

"Li'l favour? Goddammit, Gourlay, yo're askin' me to betray my employer's trust an' perjure myself!"

"The choice is yourn, Ben. The lives of yore wife an' kids agin' yore sense of honour. You gonna sacrifice them? Or are you gonna sacrifice yore conscience?" "If . . . if I do as you say, my wife an' kids'll be safe?"

"'Course."

"You . . . you'll leave us alone?"

"You have my word on that."

"Hmmm.

Benjamin Dexter sat silent for a few minutes. He had no choice. He could not, would not, sacrifice his family. Yet he continued to hesitate. If he went to the US Marshals' Office, they would surely offer him protection? But for how long? Certainly not forever, and Nathan Gourlay impressed him as a man who would be prepared to wait, for years if necessary, to fulfil his threat.

"All right," he said finally.

"You will write out and submit a fresh report, one that clears Norman Lowery of any wrong-doin'?" said Nathan Gourlay.

"Yes."

"Good! Wa'al, I reckon I'll travel along with, you, for I shall want to see it 'fore you hand it over.

"Why, don't you trust me?"

"I trust nobody, Ben."

"I shall have to work on it from the moment I hit Denver until the small hours of the morning. What shall I tell my wife? She will want to know why I didn't write it up before leavin' Mallory."

"Tell her you were anxious to git home. If you'd waited to write it up, you would have had to spend another twenty-four hours in Mallory.

"Yeah, I s'pose that'll do."

"'Course it will. Now, 'bout me seein' the report 'fore you take it into yore office, I suggest you call in at my hotel on yore way to work."

"If anyone should see me . . . "

"Yo're jest sayin' goodbye to a feller you met on the stage. What could be more innocent than that?"

"Nuthin', I guess."

"Okay. That's settled then."

Nathan Gourlay sat back and nonchalantly drank his coffee, while Benjamin Dexter found he no longer had any appetite for the pork and beans that had been placed before him.

★ ★ ★

The noon-day stage stood outside the stage line depot watched by the usual crowd of idlers. One person who did not normally have either the time or the inclination to spend in such an aimless pursuit was Brad Gourlay. Today, however, he stood on the stoop outside the Ace High Saloon and watched the stagecoach's departure. Three days earlier, he had watched its arrival and observed Benjamin Dexter dismount and walk across the street to the Land Registry office. The investigator had spent that afternoon and most of the evening in the office, thoroughly checking Norman Lowery's records. It had been almost midnight when, eventually, Dexter had retired to his room in the Grand Hotel. The following day had seen him again beavering away in the office from dawn till dusk. Now, his investigation completed, he was preparing to board the stagecoach and return to Denver.

Brad Gourlay scowled. Although Dexter had refused to confide in Norman Lowery, the rat-faced little clerk was certain that he had been rumbled. Dexter's cold and frosty attitude towards him had told him as much. Brad Gourlay prayed, therefore, that his brother would succeed in his plan. If he did not, then it would be Brad Gourlay who would be lamming out of town and aiming to cross the state line before the law caught up with him.

He watched as the passengers boarded the stagecoach. There were two railway men, travelling from Phoenix to Denver to discuss with the Governor the building of a new railroad; an elderly banker from Montrose, visiting his sister in Englewood; a grieving widow on her way from Colorado Springs to Denver, where she planned to stay with her son and his family; Benjamin Dexter and Nathan.

Brad observed that Dexter and his brother had come out of the Grand Hotel together and that Dexter, normally a cheery, freshfaced young man, was looking distinctly miserable. Dressed in a light grey city-style suit and matching Derby hat, Dexter looked exactly what he was, a nondescript little clerk. Easy game for a man of Nathan's calibre, thought Brad. As the stagecoach rattled off down Main Street, the mayor turned and pushed his way through the batwing doors, back into the Ace High Saloon. He felt in urgent need of a whiskey.

★ ★ ★

The journey from Mallory to Denver was long and tedious and, due to the chill October weather, pretty uncomfortable. Not that Benjamin Dexter noticed the discomfort. He was too wrapped up in his unhappy thoughts. He played little or no part in the general conversation inside the stagecoach and, when it halted at various staging-posts, he found he had no appetite for any refreshments. It was as though he was living a nightmare.

Eventually, however, the stagecoach arrived in Denver and drew up in front of the Last Frontier Hotel. Dexter thankfully dismounted, but, before he could retrieve his portmanteau, Nathan Gourlay sauntered over and whispered into his ear.

"I'll be stayin' at this here hotel," hissed Gourlay. "Be here with yore report first thing tomorrow mornin', 'fore you go to yore office. I'll be lookin' out for you."

"Okay."

Nathan Gourlay smiled thinly and

moved away, whereupon the clerk promptly retrieved his portmanteau and headed for home.

What should have been a happy family reunion was something of a disappointment for Dexter's wife, Anne, and his two children, seven-year-old Rachel and six-year-old Ronnie. Dexter was by no means his normal self. Usually a warm-hearted, amiable man, he greeted his wife with a perfunctory kiss and hug, and was quite off-hand with the two children. He said almost nothing about his visit to Mallory and, immediately after dinner, he retired to his study, where he proceeded to re-write his report.

It was two o'clock in the morning before he eventually came to bed, and he was up again shortly after six. Anne wanted to know why he had risen so early, for he did not usually start work until eight. He made some vague response about checking through his report before submitting it to Mr Logan, and then, after merely picking at his breakfast, he left the house. Anne watched him go, an anxious frown creasing her brow. She knew that something was wrong. Ben had been so unlike himself, and she could never before remember him leaving his breakfast practically untouched. He was always such a hearty eater.

Benjamin Dexter headed straight for the Last Frontier Hotel. His face was pale, his heart was pounding away like a demented steam-hammer and he felt quite sick. Betraying his trust was not something he did lightly. He peered up at the hotel and saw Nathan Gourlay sitting, looking out of a second-floor window. Nathan called down to the clerk to come up to Room Number Twenty-two. Slowly, reluctantly, Dexter climbed the stairs to the second floor and tapped on the door of Room Number Twenty-two. It was opened immediately.

"Come in," said the gunslinger.

Dexter stepped into the room and tossed the thin folder, which he had been carrying under his arm, onto Nathan Gourlay's bed.

"There's yore goddam report," he rasped.

Nathan grinned and picked it up. He swiftly scanned its pages. Then, when he had run his eye over the report from beginning to end, he handed it back to the whey-faced clerk.

"You've done a pretty good job, Ben," he said. "This is a report Norman Lowery can be proud of. Hell, he could git promotion on the strength of this!"

"I'm glad yo're satisfied."

"Oh, I am, Ben; I am."

"An' you'll leave my family alone?"

"That was the deal."

"You swear it?"

"I swear it, Ben."

"Okay." Benjamin Dexter clutched the report and turned to go. "You . . . you'll be leavin' town then?" he said, as he paused on the threshold.

"On the next stage," said Nathan Gourlay.

The gunslinger rose and slapped on his black Derby hat, and began to follow Dexter out of the room.

"The next stage ain't till noon," said Dexter.

"I know, but I reckon I'll mosey along with you as far as yore office. Jest to make sure you an' yore report git there safely," replied Nathan Gourlay, with a sardonic grin.

Benjamin Dexter shrugged his shoulders.

"If you must," he said dolefully.

The two men walked slowly along Main Street. A cold wind blew and the sky was grey and overcast, threatening rain. But Benjamin Dexter was impervious to the weather. He was totally immersed in the misery of his situation. An honest, trustworthy man, he was wracked with guilt.

The genial greeting from his boss, Sam Logan, did nothing to ease matters. Dexter's conscience bade him own up to what he had done. Yet he dared not. If he did so, he would be putting the lives of his wife and children at risk. Therefore, he handed over the false report to Logan.

"Wa'al, Ben," said Logan, a small, baldheaded man, with twinkling blue eyes and a rosy red face, "How'd it go? You find what we expected?"

"Nope. The Mallory office's records are in apple pie order."

"So, Norman Lowery is in the clear?"

"Yup."

"Wa'al, I'll be darned!" Logan scratched his head and glanced up from behind his desk at his young associate. "I must say I'm real surprised, though naturally I'm pleased an' relieved. After all, 'tain't very nice when a colleague is suspected of falsifyin' official records."

"Nope."

"An' yo're sure everythin's above board?"

"Yes, Mr Logan. It is all in my report."

"Okay. Thanks, Ben. I'll . . . er . . . I'll study it."

"Yessir."

Once Dexter had left his office, Sam Logan opened the folder and began to read. The report was clear and succinct, and it certainly cleared Norman Lowery of any misdemeanour. Yet Logan felt uneasy. It was almost too good to be true, and, into the bargain, Benjamin Dexter, who was usually a cheerful young man, had this morning looked distinctly unhappy. Why, wondered Logan, when having absolved Norman Lowery from guilt, the young man should have been positively euphoric? Logan debated whether or not to call Dexter back into his office, but he was prevented from so doing by a summons from Denver's mayor to an emergency town council meeting, for, in addition to managing the Land Registry office, Logan was also a town councillor. Therefore, he had no choice other than to shelve the matter. Consequently, he placed the report in his safe, intending to discuss it with Dexter on the following morning.

Only when he was completely satisfied, would he submit it to the Governor. It was, after all, Governor Bill Watson who had initiated the investigation.

For Benjamin Dexter that Friday was the longest day of his young life, but, somehow or other, he got through it. Still torn with guilt and remorse, he left the office at five o'clock. However, he did not head for home, as he had done on every other working day of his married life. Instead, he made his way along the sidewalk to the Prairie Dog Saloon.

Dexter rarely drank and, when he did, he invariably stuck to beer. On this occasion, though, he ordered a whiskey and told the bartender to leave the bottle. Max Barton, who owned the Prairie Dog, raised a surprised eyebrow, but did not intervene. Providing Dexter paid for his drink, the saloon-keeper was not about to dissuade him from drowning his sorrows.

It was, therefore, an extremely drunk Benjamin Dexter who eventually staggered out of the saloon at half-past-ten on that murky October evening. The rain, that had been threatening to fall all day, had finally arrived. Dexter turned up his collar and tottered off along the sidewalk. In his drunken stupor, he had come to a decision, one which he would, in all probability, rescind in the cold light of the following morning. He had decided that he would confess everything to Sam Logan, and then he and his family would immediately leave Denver and head East. As for Nathan Gourlay, the villain would surely never find him, not so long as he was careful to cover his tracks? This was the conclusion to which Dexter had come and, in consequence, he was in a much happier frame of mind than when he had entered the Prairie Dog.

There were few people about, the rain having driven most of them indoors. Therefore, Dexter had the sidewalk to himself. He staggered on through the downpour until he reached Mae

Shipton's bordello. There he found his way barred, not by one of Mae Shipton's girls, but by a tall, lean man in a long black leather coat. The light from the bordello's open doorway spilled out onto the sidewalk and lit up the man's face. Dexter stared at it and gasped.

"Gourlay!" he cried. "I thought you were leavin' on the noon-day stage?"

"I lied," said Nathan Gourlay quietly.

"But . . . but why?"

"I got me some unfinished business."

"I . . . I don't understand."

"I cain't let you live. S'pose you decide to renege on our li'l deal?" rasped Gourlay.

"But . . . but I wouldn't!" exclaimed Dexter.

"I've had my eye on you all evenin'. You've been drinkin' heavily, an' now yo're good 'n' drunk. Wa'al, drunks can be mighty unreliable."

"I . . . I ain't unreliable. Honest, Mr Gourlay, I . . . "

Dexter got no further. As he spoke,

Nathan Gourlay suddenly grabbed him, and dragged him off the sidewalk and up the narrow alley that lay between the bordello and the Last Frontier Hotel. Then, while the rain continued to beat down relentlessly, Gourlay spun him round, rammed a knee into the small of his back and slammed a forearm across the front of his throat.

"So long, Dexter," hissed Gourlay.

"No-o-o-o!"

Benjamin Dexter's cry was cut short, for Nathan Gourlay swiftly, viciously, jerked the clerk's head back and broke his neck, as easily as he might snap a twig.

The murderer smiled thinly. He had not, as he had stated, been observing Dexter all evening. To have done so would have been to risk detection. However, from time to time during the course of the evening, Nathan had glanced over the batwing doors of the Prairie Dog Saloon and, each time he had looked in, Dexter had been propped up against the bar

quietly consuming his bottle of red-
eye. Subsequently, Nathan had kept
a careful watch from the window
of another saloon, the Red Garter,
fifty yards down Main Street on the
opposite side. And, when Dexter had
finally tottered out of the Prairie Dog,
Nathan Gourlay had downed his drink
and quickly made his way across the
street, intending to intercept the Land
Registry clerk outside Mae Shipton's
bordello. This he had done, and now
all that remained to be done was to
dispose of Benjamin Dexter's body.

Gourlay slung the dead man over
his shoulder and grinned. He realised
he had been lucky. The torrential rain
had emptied Denver's Main Street and,
so, enabled him to pull Dexter into
the blackness of the alleyway without
fear of being seen by any of the
townsfolk. He stared at the steep
flight of wooden steps leading up from
the alley to a narrow, second-floor
door, a secluded side-entrance to the
bordello. This door, Gourlay guessed,

was probably reserved for the use of those of Denver's more prominent citizens who patronised Mae Shipton's establishment, yet had no wish that anyone should know. A couple of quick dashes in and out of the alleyway was all that was needed when they paid the bordello a clandestine visit.

Slowly, Nathan Gourlay mounted the steps. Eventually, thankfully, he reached the top. He paused for breath, for, although not a big man, Benjamin Dexter was no light weight. Gourlay stood him upright and then pushed him backwards down the stairway. Dexter's corpse bounced off each and every step until finally it ended up in a heap at the bottom. Gourlay followed it down and stepped negligently over it on his way out into Main Street. He could see the report in tomorrow's newspaper:

'Drunken Land Registry Clerk Falls To His Death.
Last night, Benjamin Dexter, a clerk at Denver's Office of Land Registry,

enjoyed a binge at the Prairie Dog Saloon and then attempted to enter Mae Shipton's establishment by a side entrance. Unfortunately, in his drunken stupor, he fell down the stairway leading up to the side entrance and broke his neck, killing himself.'

Gourlay laughed harshly. He had told Brad that he would take care of the matter of Dexter's investigation, and he had done just that. Brad would find him a useful man to have around.

He made his way to the livery stables, where he had stabled the black mare he had bought that morning. He saddled her and paid the hostler his dues. Then he rode off through the pouring rain, up Main Street and out past the town limits. It was going to be a long, wet ride back to Mallory.

3

CHIEF Marshall Frank Wayne was not looking forward to his interview that morning with Anne Dexter. A big, spare man with grizzled grey hair and a lean, craggy face, he had no qualms about facing the wildest of outlaws, the deadliest of gunslingers, or the most ruthless of renegades. But he had no wish to face Benjamin Dexter's grieving young widow. He did not know how to deal with a woman's tears. They made him feel embarrassed and uncomfortable.

However, when she was shown into his private office at the US Marshals' Headquarters, Anne Dexter was not weeping. The time for crying was over. She wanted her husband's murderer brought to justice, and she knew that she must remain in control of herself.

Dark-haired and petite, Anne was

a pretty woman, and she seemed particularly lovely to the Chief Marshal, as she stood on the threshold of his office, pale-faced and anxious-looking.

"Come on in, Mrs Dexter," he said, hastily rising to greet her and fetch her a chair. Then, when they were both seated, he behind his large mahogany desk and his visitor in front of it, Frank Wayne began by saying, "Despite yore conviction that yore husband was murdered, I'm afraid I can find no evidence that his death was anythin' other than accidental."

"You believe Ben was drunk an' went in search of a whore, an' that he simply tumbled down that stairway at the side of Mae Shipton's place, don't you?" she said quietly.

Chief Marshal Wayne nodded.

"'Fraid so, ma'am," he said.

"But Ben didn't hardly ever drink. An' he was a happily married man. Why in tarnation would he want a whore for the night?" demanded Anne.

"I dunno. But he won't be the first,

or the last, married man to fancy slippin' 'tween the sheets with someone other than his wife," commented Wayne.

"No, Marshal, I cain't accept that. Ben would never . . . " But Anne could not bear to finish the sentence. "He wasn't his usual self y'know, when he came back from Mallory," she said firmly.

"I know. You already told me."

"There was somethin' wrong. I'm convinced of it."

"Connected, you reckon, with this enquiry he made in Mallory?"

"Yes."

"Wa'al, I had a word with Sam Logan, and he seemed satisfied with yore husband's report."

"Ben exonerated a man suspected of falsifying Land Registry records. Surely this was a cause for rejoicin', yet Ben seemed deeply depressed?"

"Yeah; Mr Logan said much the same. But, hell, yore husband had jest completed one helluva long stagecoach ride an' then, on yore own admission, he spent most of the night writin' up his report, so mebbe he was simply plumb tuckered out?"

"No: it was more than that. I know it." Anne's eyes glittered angrily and she asked, "Have you checked with Ben's fellow-passengers on the stagecoach? Mebbe one or other of them could offer you some kind of clue?"

"We're clutchin' at straws here, ma'am."

"Surely it's worth a try?"

"I've already spoken with most of the folk who got off the stagecoach here in Denver. A coupla railroad men an' a widow like yoreself. The other feller, who got off here, seems to have high-tailed it outta town. Bought hisself a black mare an' left on the very night yore husband fell to his death."

"That's suspicious!"

"Aw, come on, ma'am! Folks ride in an' outta Denver all the time."

"Even so."

"There ain't nuthin' to connect that feller, or any of the other passengers on

54

that stage, with yore husband's death. I questioned 'em pretty darned closely, an' they reckon yore husband hardly said a word to anyone durin' the course of the entire journey."

"That's downright peculiar, for Ben was usually a pretty friendly, talkative kinda guy."

"Wa'al, that's it, I'm afraid."

"Couldn't you send one of yore men to Mallory, to check up an' sniff around an' . . . ?"

"What's the point? We know what yore husband was doin' there. It's all in his report."

"But, Marshal, I jest know my husband was murdered!"

"You may know it, Mrs Dexter, but you cain't prove it. There ain't a single shred of evidence to suggest that yore husband was anythin' but a victim of his own inebriation." Frank Wayne gazed sympathetically at the widow and added quietly, "I'm sorry, but there ain't no more I can do."

Anne Dexter nodded. Pale as a

ghost, she rose from her chair. She had been afraid that the US marshals' investigation would come to nothing, yet she felt instinctively that Ben had not climbed those stairs to the side-door of the bordello. There was no question that he had been drunk. Nevertheless, drunk or sober, he would never have gone in search of a whore. The question was, what on earth had driven him to drink? Anne was determined to find out. Chief Marshal Frank Wayne might have closed his enquiry, but she had certainly not given up hers.

"Thank you for yore trouble, Marshal," she said stiffly and, turning on her heel, she stalked out of his office.

Wayne half-rose, then subsided again onto his chair behind the mahogany desk. He sincerely regretted he had been unable to help. But he had an office to run and law and order to maintain state-wide. Therefore, he could not afford to waste any more time upon what he considered to be

Anne Dexter's unreasonable obsession. He sighed deeply and began to study the papers which lay before him on his desk.

* * *

It was two o'clock in the afternoon and the Governor of Colorado had lunched well. Usually, he snatched a light bite and carried on with his duties of office. But today was different. Today he was entertaining an old friend who had unexpectedly called upon him.

The two men sat in the Governor's parlour, relaxing together and enjoying some fine old French brandy, which the Governor kept for very special occasions indeed. But, then, it was seven years since the two men had last seen each other. That was when their regiment had disbanded at the end of the Civil War and Lieutenant Bill Watson and Sergeant Jack Stone had shaken hands and ridden off in different directions. In those seven years, both men had changed considerably. No longer were they the two raw young greenhorns who had enlisted together and then fought together for the Union.

Governor Bill Watson was a tall, blondhaired man, handsome and urbane. He had taken to politics like a duck takes to water. His ascent had been rapid, and now he was governor of one of the Union's most prosperous states. He had married a senator's daughter and this had done his political advancement no harm whatsoever. In his white linen three-piece suit and shiny black shoes, he looked every inch the part. He enjoyed the cut and thrust of politics, the responsibilities and the power his office gave him, and he was comfortable with himself. He had achieved much and he was not averse to saying so.

Jack Stone, on the other hand, had had a pretty rough ride during those seven years. Indeed, he had had one helluva tough time since way back, when he was a kid in Kentucky.

His father had lost the family farm through his gambling and had then died in a bar-room brawl. Thereafter, his mother had struggled, alone and unaided, to bring up her young son. Stone was fourteen years old when, worn out by her efforts, his mother had died.

Now on his own, he had tried most things: farm work, ranch work, riding herd on cattle-drives, a little bronco-busting, and then, during the Civil War, some soldiering. After the war, he had served with the army for a while as an Indian scout. But the white man's savagery towards his red brother had sickened Stone and he had resigned.

Following this, the Kentuckian had been taken on as a hand at the Bar JV ranch, just outside Henderson in Nevada. There he had married, but, before the marriage was one year old, his young wife had died in childbirth, with the child stillborn. This tragic event had had a devastating effect upon him and Stone had taken to the bottle. It was some months before he recovered, but, by then, he was a changed man; a man who had been forged by the fire of bitter experience, and a man who was fated to be forever moving on.

His reputation with a gun had been earned subsequently, with a series of jobs such as guard on the Overland stage, deputy US marshal and deputy sheriff. At present, Stone was between jobs and was considering prospecting for gold. It was for this purpose that he had ridden south to Colorado, and, having heard that his old comrade-in-arms had become State Governor, he had naturally enough called in to see him on his way to the goldfields.

Time had not been as kind to Jack Stone as it had to Governor Bill Watson. The Kentuckian was twenty-seven years old, yet looked at least ten years older. Six-foot two-inches in his stocking feet and consisting of nigh on two hundred pounds of muscle and bone, he bore the scars, both mental and physical, of his turbulent and often unhappy life. The bullet holes had healed, but the broken nose remained and the emotional wounds, which had made Stone what he was, would never completely heal. His square-cut face was deeply lined and his thick brown hair liberally flecked with grey.

Stone wore a red kerchief round his thick, strong neck, a knee-length buckskin jacket over his grey shirt, faded denim pants over unspurred boots and, tied down on his right thigh, a Frontier Model Colt. He looked, and was, a hard man to cross.

Bill Watson had cancelled all engagements for the rest of the day, and he and Stone were happily reminiscing while they sipped their brandies and puffed away contentedly on the Governor's excellent cigars. Stone was enjoying the unaccustomed comfort, his cool blue eyes twinkled merrily and a wide smile lightened his craggy countenance. He was in mid-sentence when, unexpectedly, they were interrupted by a quiet tap on the parlour door.

Bill Watson looked less than pleased at the interruption, but felt he could not ignore it. Consequently, he called out, "Come in."

A tall, nervous-looking young man entered. He was smartly dressed in a grey three-piece suit and was the Governor's private secretary, Nat Hepburn.

"Sorry to disturb you, Governor," said Hepburn, glancing anxiously from Watson to the Kentuckian and back again.

"Wa'al, what is it?" demanded Watson.

"It . . . it's Mrs Dexter. You know, her husband was killed a coupla days back, fell down the stairs outside . . . "

"Yeah, yeah, I know," said Watson testily.

"She . . . she's demandin' to see you."

"Is she indeed?"

"Yeah. She came up to the house

62

just 'fore you sat down to lunch. I said you couldn't be disturbed, but she elected to wait. She's been sittin' out in the hall for well over two hours now. She says she won't go until she's spoken with you."

"Goddammit!" Watson frowned and shrugged his broad shoulders resignedly. "Okay, Nat, I s'pose you'd better bring her in," he sighed.

"Thank you, sir. I'll go fetch her," said a relieved Nat Hepburn.

Bill Watson glanced over at his visitor.

"Sorry 'bout this, Jack," he said.

"That's okay," said Stone. "What's her beef, d'you reckon?"

"Wa'al, it's a long story. Guess I'd best begin at the beginnin'. There's been some disturbin' rumours comin' outta the goldfields of prospectors havin' vanished an' their claims subsequently bein' worked by the Mallory Minin' Company, a company owned by one Brad Gourlay, the mayor over at Mallory. Consequently, I asked Sam

Logan, at the Office of Land Registry here in Denver, to send one of his most trusted employees to Mallory, to examine the records held in the branch office there."

"An' he sent Mrs Dexter's husband?"

"Right."

"An' . . . ?"

"An' nuthin'. Ben Dexter returned, givin' the Mallory office a clean bill of health. The same night he got hisself real drunk at the Prairie Dog Saloon an' didn't go home. Next mornin', he was found dead at the foot of the stairway leadin' up to the second-floor side-entrance of Mae Shipton's bordello. Seemed he'd fallen down the steps an' broken his neck."

"So, what does Mrs Dexter want you to do 'bout it, Bill?"

"I dunno exactly. She's been over to the US Marshals' Office demandin' an investigation. She reckons her husband's death wasn't no accident, y'see."

"Why in tarnation should she think that?"

"Wa'al," began Bill Watson, but he got no further, for, at that very moment, his secretary ushered in the widow.

Both men rose hastily to their feet and Watson quickly offered Anne Dexter a chair. She sat down on the edge of it, her face pale and anxious, but with a determined look in her sad brown eyes. The Governor glanced towards his secretary and nodded.

"Okay, Nat, that'll be all," said Watson. He waited until Nat Hepburn had left the room, and then he turned and asked the widow, "Wa'al, Mrs Dexter, what can I do for you?"

"I want you to help me track down my husband's murderer," replied the widow quietly.

"Yore husband's murderer? But Chief Marshal Wayne informs me that there was nuthin' to suggest his death was anythin' other than accidental."

"I know."

"Wa'al, then?"

"Chief Marshal Wayne is wrong."

"But . . ."

"You sent Ben to Mallory, Governor."

"I asked Sam Logan to send somebody he could trust. He chose to send Ben."

"To investigate the Land Registry office over in Mallory?"

"Yes. Which he did. An' he reported back that, contrary to my expectations, the records there were in apple-pie order."

"Ben didn't want the job, y'know. It ain't very nice checkin' up on one of yore colleagues."

"No, I guess not."

"So, you'd think he'd have been pleased to find the records were in order."

"I s'pose."

"Wa'al, he wasn't. Not in the least."

"That's sure odd," interjected Stone.

"As was his behaviour on his return from Mallory. He was quite unlike his usual self."

"Indeed?" Stone frowned and asked, "Would you mind tellin' us exactly what yore husband did, an' how he behaved, between arrivin' back from Mallory an' bein' found dead outside Mae Shipton's bordello?"

Anne Dexter concentrated her gaze upon the Kentuckian. She eyed him with unconcealed curiosity.

"I don't think I've had the pleasure . . . ?" she began.

"Stone's the name. Jack Stone. I'm an old buddy of the Governor."

"I see." Anne glanced at the Governor. "Is it all right if I tell him?" she asked.

"Of course it is. You can trust Jack implicitly," said Watson.

The widow nodded and went on to relate the events as they had occurred. She spoke slowly and precisely and was gratified to see that she had both men's undivided attention. When she had finished, Stone took a long draw on his cigar. Then he leant back in his chair and closed his eyes. He meditated in this manner for some moments.

"Mebbe, after all, yore husband

didn't find them there records to be in order," he said finally.

"But his report . . . "

"He could have been got at."

"Ben was as honest as the day is long!" exclaimed Anne indignantly.

"There are many ways of persuadin' a feller to do somethin' he doesn't wanta do," said Stone.

"What are you suggestin', Jack?" enquired Watson.

"I'm suggestin' he was warned not to expose any discrepancies he might have found at the Land Registry office in Mallory."

"By whom?"

"By that there Brad Gourlay you told me 'bout. Or by someone on Gourlay's pay-roll."

"Mr Stone's right!" cried Anne. "That's it! If 'n' he was threatened . . . "

"With what?" asked Watson.

"I dunno. Mebbe Gourlay threatened to kill me or the kids. Ben would've done anythin' to protect his family."

"Even to the extent of falsifyin' his

report?" said Watson.

"Reckon so."

"But he'd have sure felt as guilty as hell. Right, Mrs Dexter?" said Stone.

"Yes, Ben was always terribly conscientious. He would have hated to betray the trust that had been placed in him."

"Which could explain his depression an' the heavy drinkin'."

"But not his death," said Anne.

"Unless he did fall down them stairs?" said Watson.

"No! Never! I'm convinced Ben had no intention of visitin' that bordello. My guess is, he was murdered, then thrown down the bordello steps to make it look like an accident."

"That's possible. Suppose one of Brad Gourlay's men travelled with him on the stage?" suggested Stone.

"That feller who high-tailed it outta town on the very night Ben died!" cried Anne.

"What feller?" asked Watson.

"Chief Marshal Wayne told me that

one of the passengers, who got out here in Denver, left town 'bout the time Ben was killed."

"If 'n' he did murder Mrs Dexter's husband, an' he is on Brad Gourlay's pay-roll, then I guess he probably headed straight back to Mallory," said Stone.

"This is pure supposition!" objected Watson.

"So, you got a better theory, Governor?" demanded Anne.

"No. Guess not."

"Then, will you instruct Chief Marshal Wayne to send one of his men over to Mallory, to search for an' arrest that feller?"

"I don't think so," said the Governor.

"But . . . ?"

"Let's jest s'pose yo're right, an' we git a good description of the feller on the stage. An' the marshal finds him in Mallory. Then what? He cain't hardly arrest him simply 'cause he happened to leave town on the same night yore husband died."

"I don't see why not."

"'Cause we ain't got no evidence that he murdered yore husband. Indeed, there ain't no evidence that yore husband was murdered. Like I said, it's all pure supposition."

"So, you ain't gonna do nuthin'?"

"I didn't say that."

"Wa'al, what are you gonna do?"

"I cain't initiate an official investigation, that's for sure. However, mebbe I could send an undercover agent to Mallory?" Bill Watson smiled wryly and turned to face Jack Stone. "You said you was reckonin' on doin' a li'l prospectin', didn't yuh, Jack?" he murmured.

"Yeah," said the Kentuckian.

"Prospectin' for gold is a mighty chancey business," commented Watson.

"Always has been," agreed Stone.

"So, hows about combinin' yore prospectin' with a li'l investigative work? That way you cain't lose. If 'n' you don't strike it rich, at least you'll be earnin' decent wages."

"You aimin' to pay me outta state funds, then?"

"Yup. If you'll take on the job. Them railroad men are still in town. I can git them to give us a description of that feller who travelled with Ben Dexter from Mallory an' then lammed outta town on the night he died. So, whaddya say?"

Jack Stone puffed thoughtfully on his cigar. What Bill Watson said about prospecting for gold was true. But, assuming that their supposition was right and Brad Gourlay was behind Ben Dexter's murder, then investigating Mallory's mayor could prove to be a darned risky business. In fact, Stone reckoned he might not live to collect his wages.

"I ain't gonna work for peanuts, not even to oblige you, Bill," he said.

"Didn't 'spect you would. You'll git the same pay as a US marshal for the duration of the enquiry," promised the Governor.

"That seems fair."

"Then, you'll take on the investigation, Mr Stone," asked Anne Dexter, gazing imploringly at the Kentuckian.

Stone smiled at the widow.

"Guess so, ma'am," he drawled.

4

THE ride to Mallory was complicated by the fact that Stone's friend, the Governor, had warned him that a Pawnee renegade, by the name of Red Lynx, was on the rampage, terrorising the territory, and that he, Stone, had best keep his eyes peeled.

It seemed Red Lynx was not some ambitious young buck keen to establish himself as a potential chief, capable of leading the Pawnee nation to war against the white man. He was simply a ruthless, bloodthirsty savage, who, with a band of a dozen like-minded braves, attacked lone travellers and isolated homesteads, killing the men and even the children, raping the women, and stealing their stock, weapons, ammunition and, if any existed, their whiskey.

In consequence of Bill Watson's warning, Jack Stone kept clear of the main trail and carefully avoided riding through anywhere where the redskins might be lying in ambush. This necessitated the Kentuckian making various detours and added a couple of days to his journey. Eventually, however, he reached Mallory, having seen neither hide nor hair of Red Lynx and his war-party.

Having booked a room at the Grand Hotel, the Kentuckian observed sourly that Brad Gourlay's establishment, a dilapidated, two-storey frame building with peeling white paint and a large population of cockroaches, was most inaptly named. Nevertheless, since it was Mallory's only hotel, he had no choice other than to book in there. And he had his bay gelding taken care of at the livery stables also owned by the mayor. Then, he made his way over to the Ace High Saloon.

A cold wind whistled down Main Street and there was a hint of rain in the air. Stone had turned up the collar of his buckskin jacket. Thankfully, he stepped through the batwing doors and into the fuggy warmth of the saloon. It was early evening, but already the saloon was doing brisk business. There was a crowd round the roulette wheel, all the blackjack tables were surrounded by eager gamblers, and half-a-dozen poker games were in progress. Nancy Carson's girls, too, were being kept busy, and the drinkers standing round the bar were three to four deep.

Stone threaded his way through the tables to the bar. He walked slowly and deliberately, noting the lay-out of the saloon, with its wooden stairway leading up to a railed walkway that ran the entire length of one side. It was from off this walkway that the saloon girls and their customers disappeared into the various bedrooms.

The Kentuckian had been well-briefed by Bill Watson and knew who to look out for. He pushed through the throng of drinkers at the bar and ordered a beer. Then he waited. But he did not have long to wait, for he had barely tasted his second beer before four men entered through the batwing doors and strolled across the saloon towards the bar.

Jack Stone eyed them carefully from his vantage point, propped against the hammered copper bar-top. The fat, ruddy-faced lawman was easily identifiable, since he was wearing his tin star. Joe Banks and the tall, thin man dressed all in black, whom Stone took to be the gunslinger, Long Tom Russell, followed hard upon the heels of two smartly dressed individuals, one of whom was sporting a bright crimson velvet vest. The other's attire exactly accorded with the description given to Stone of that worn by Benjamin Dexter's mysterious travelling companion. Stone guessed that the man in the crimson vest was Mallory's mayor, Brad Gourlay. The other man was undoubtedly his brother, for the likeness was unmistakable. Stone smiled wryly. No mention had been made of any brother.

As they approached the bar, the four men veered to their left and entered a small office, which was set to one side of the bar-counter. Immediately, Nancy Carson despatched one of her bartenders after them. He carried a tray, bearing four glasses and a bottle of her best whiskey, into the office and returned with only the tray.

Stone remained in the Ace High Saloon for a couple of hours or more, but neither Brad Gourlay nor any of his three companions emerged from the office. Stone's time was not entirely wasted, however, for he picked up a fair amount of local gossip, learning that Brad Gourlay's brother was called Nathan and was a fairly recent arrival in Mallory. He also learned that Gourlay had the town pretty much sewn up. Nobody actually said anything against Brad Gourlay. Stone figured they dared not. Nevertheless, he got the impression that the mayor was not universally loved.

A hot meal in the dining-room at the Grand Hotel and Stone was ready to retire for the night. It was as well that his day in the saddle had exhausted him, otherwise he might have had some trouble getting off to sleep. Although it was almost midnight when, eventually, Stone returned to his hotel room, there was no sign of the town quietening down. Drunks reeled from saloon to bordello and back again, shouting, singing and shooting off their six-guns. This went on right through the small hours until dawn. Consequently, the Kentuckian was woken from his slumbers from time to time, and fell into a final sleep only when the morning rains came and the last drunk had tottered off home.

★ ★ ★

The hammering on his bedroom door was loud and persistent. Jack Stone opened a bleary eye. The rain beat furiously against the window panes and he was tempted to turn over. But the knocking continued unabated. Wearily, Stone clambered out of bed. He grabbed his Frontier Model Colt from its holster, crossed the room and threw open the door.

Sheriff Joe Banks blinked and stepped back a couple of paces. He had not expected to find himself looking down the barrel of a forty-five calibre revolver. He pointed a nervous finger at Stone's gun.

"Hey . . . hey, put that there gun away!" he gasped.

"You gonna make me?" growled Stone.

"Now, lookee here, I'm the law around these parts an' . . . "

"Okay, Sheriff, so what can I do for you?" asked the Kentuckian, lowering, but not relinquishing, the gun.

"I . . . I always check up on any newcomers in town. Like to know who we've got here in Mallory," said Banks.

Stone smiled. Bill Wilson had told

him that Mallory welcomed any riff-raff, providing they had money to burn. So, the sheriff could hardly be worried about keeping undesirables out of town. Stone decided, therefore, to conceal his true identity. He had a certain reputation and he had no wish that Banks should know he had, in his time, been a lawman.

"Wa'al, my name's Smith. John Smith," he said, unwittingly adopting the same pseudonym as that used by Nathan Gourlay when he introduced himself to Benjamin Dexter.

"Howdy, Mr Smith. Welcome to Mallory. I hope you enjoy yore stay," said Banks amiably. He had quickly determined to use a friendly approach, for the big Kentuckian looked to be a pretty tough customer, and the Frontier Model Colt grasped in his right hand made the sheriff more than a little nervous. "You stayin' in town or jest passin' through?" he asked.

"Ain't rightly sure," said Stone. "Depends."

"On what?"

"On how things pan out."

"So, what are you aimin' on doin' here in Mallory?"

"Heard the territory round about is rich with gold. Reckon I might try me a li'l prospectin'."

"I see. You done any prospectin' before, Mr Smith?"

"Nope."

"Then, you won't have no equipment, nor provisions, I guess?"

"That's right."

"Wa'al, you'll git the best deal in Brad Gourlay's general store, straight across the street."

"I'll bear that in mind," promised Stone.

"You do that," said Banks.

"Yeah. Wa'al, if that's all, Sheriff, I'd like to grab me a coupla more hours' sleep," said the Kentuckian. "Is that okay by you?"

"Yeah, that's fine by me. I'll be moseyin' along. See you around, Mr Smith."

Stone smiled wryly and slowly closed the bedroom door. To prevent Banks from becoming suspicious, he would have to ride out into the hills and start prospecting for gold, just as he had planned to do before his meeting with the Governor. But that would mean leaving Mallory, and Stone's investigation required him to remain in town. He cursed beneath his breath. Then he glanced out of the window at the torrential rain splashing down and turning Main Street into a river of mud. While the rain fell, he had an excuse for remaining in town. He determined, therefore, to make the most of his time in Mallory and, so, rather reluctantly forewent his further two hours in bed.

Following breakfast in the hotel dining-room, Stone set out on a tour of the town's three saloons. He quickly found that, even during the morning and afternoon, they enjoyed a pretty brisk trade. There always seemed to be a fair crowd anxious to drink, gamble or fornicate their hours away. Stone, for his part, was careful to drink sparingly as, in turn, he surveyed the scene at each saloon. He smoked his way through a plentiful supply of cheroots, however. How many days would he have to do this before he picked up something of real interest, he wondered?

That night he slept badly. He realised he had no proper plan of campaign. Wandering round Mallory's three saloons, hoping to find some incriminating evidence against the Gourlay brothers, was, he conceded, pretty hopeless. But what else could he do? He knew that, should the rain cease, he would have to head for the hills. Could he then, in all honesty, take the wages the Governor had promised him.

After a short deliberation, Stone decided that, whatever the weather, he would continue his perambulations round town for two days more. Then, if he had learned nothing that might help his enquiry, he would go over to the stage line depot and telegraph the Governor, advising him that he proposed to abandon the investigation. That done, he would purchase the necessary equipment and provisions, ride out into the hills and try his hand at prospecting for gold. Stone was not at all happy at the idea of failing his friend and letting down Benjamin Dexter's widow. Nevertheless, he felt he could not continue to wander aimlessly round Mallory for much longer.

In the event, the arrival of Wally O'Brien on the following morning gave the Kentuckian the break that he needed.

Wally O'Brien was a small, chirpy man in his late sixties. His deeply lined, weatherbeaten face was partially hidden behind a silvery white beard and drooping moustache. A shock of silvery white hair, as thick as it had been when he was still a boy, protruded from beneath his raccoon-skin hat, while, beneath a coat cobbled together from a remarkable variety of furs, he was clad entirely in buckskins, even down to the moccasins he wore on his feet. He rode a decrepit-looking grey mare and led a heavily-laden mule. His faded blue eyes twinkled merrily and he sang lustily, in a croaking, off-key voice, the words of the old Irish ballad, "When Irish Eyes Are Smiling."

The old-timer had been a gold prospector for almost all of his adult life. In fact, he had been one of the first to rush up into the Klondike. But, until now, he had never struck it lucky. The little gold he had found had been no more than sufficient to keep him alive. Now, however, in a small creek three miles north of Mallory, O'Brien had found a rich seam. He was all set to become a very rich man indeed.

He tethered the mare and the mule to the hitching-post in front of Al Cooney's Jack of Diamonds Saloon and climbed up onto the stoop. But he did not enter the saloon. Instead, he trotted along the sidewalk to the Land Registry office, went inside and proceeded to register his claim.

"Ain't gonna have nobody jump this claim. No, sirree!" he informed Norman Lowery.

The clerk eyed him curiously from behind his steel-rimmed spectacles.

"You struck it lucky, then?" he enquired.

"You bet. I'm gonna be a rich man, mister."

"Really?"

"Yeah. This is the big one! An' I should know. Been prospectin' for more years 'n I care to remember."

"Wa'al, congratulations, sir."

Norman Lowery smiled pleasantly at the prospector and set to registering O'Brien's claim. Then, when the business was done and Wally O'Brien was on his way back to the Jack of Diamonds, where he intended to buy himself a few celebratory drinks, Lowery closed the office and headed for Brad Gourlay's Ace High Saloon.

Wally O'Brien's arrival in town had not gone unremarked. His singing had seen to that. And, among those who had watched his cheerful progress up the muddy thoroughfare to the Jack of Diamonds, was the Kentuckian, Jack Stone.

Stone did not have to be much of a detective to guess that here was a prospector who had struck it rich. Immediately, he strapped on his gun-belt, shrugged on his buckskin jacket and, scooping up his grey Stetson, left the hotel room and clattered downstairs.

Outside, he shivered for a few moments in the chill wind. The rain had ceased, but the skies remained grey and overcast. There was no sign of Wally O'Brien. However, Stone could hardly miss observing the prospector's mare and mule tethered to the rail outside the Jack of Diamonds. He smiled and headed across Main Street towards the saloon, carefully picking his way through the mud. He mounted the half-a-dozen steps up onto the stoop and went in through the batwing doors.

The Jack of Diamonds was little different to Brad Gourlay's Ace High, except that it was rather less crowded. A few poker games were in progress, carried on from the night before, some early morning drinkers stood slumped across the bar and those customers who had spent the night with Al Cooney's girls stumped wearily downstairs.

Stone went over to the bar and ordered a beer. Then he lit a cheroot and, propping himself against the bar-counter, awaited events. He had not long to wait before Wally O'Brien put in an appearance. The old-timer, having registered his claim, was anxious to celebrate his lucky strike. Indeed, he was soon telling all and sundry about how he had finally struck it rich, and was happily buying the circle of listeners a round of drinks.

It was as he ordered a second round that Brad Gourlay walked into the saloon. The mayor seemed to be totally unaware of Wally O'Brien's presence. He stopped here and there to have a word with various acquaintances. Then, when eventually he reached the bar, he ignored the crowd round the prospector, ordered himself a drink and began a conversation with Al Cooney. But Stone, at the opposite end of the bar, was not fooled. He had no doubt that Brad Gourlay had hurried across to the Jack of Diamonds for the express purpose of checking up on Wally O'Brien. Stone surreptitiously watched the mayor and waited for him to make his move.

Eventually, as the Kentuckian had guessed he would, Brad Gourlay turned and, slowly pushing his way through the circle of drinkers, addressed the by-now-quite-merry prospector.

"I couldn't help overhearin' you, sir," he boomed. "It would appear you have struck gold in a big way."

"Sure have," agreed O'Brien amiably.

"Wa'al, congratulations."

"Thank you."

"You will doubtless be requirin' some provisions?"

"That's the reason I'm in town. Or at least one reason."

"The other, I guess, is to register your claim?"

"Yessir."

"A wise move, my friend. There are some most dishonest folks about these days. I rejoice that you have had the good sense to protect yoreself from any of those who might wish to jump yore claim. Have you already registered?"

"I have."

"Splendid! Splendid! Wa'al, my name's Brad Gourlay an', besides bein' mayor of this here town, I own the general store across the street. So, if it's provisions you want, I reckon you cain't do better than drop into my li'l establishment. You won't git cheaper prices anywhere in Mallory. Ain't that right, Al?"

The saloon-keeper nodded. He dared not say otherwise.

"That's right," he muttered.

"So, when are you aimin' on headin'

back to yore claim?" enquired Gourlay casually.

"First light tomorrow," said Wally O'Brien. "I'm gonna rest up in town for a few hours. Then, tonight, I figure on havin' me some fun. Reckon I'll down a few whiskies, enjoy a good hot meal an' git myself a woman for the night."

"Wa'al, when yo're good 'n' ready, jest mosey along to the Ace High. I'll have a word with Nancy Carson an' tell her to fix you up with one of her girls, one who'll be sure to pander to yore ev'ry wish."

"That's mighty civil of you, sir."

"Not at all. Not at all. I'm a feller who likes to lend a helpin' hand."

With these words, Brad Gourlay shook the prospector warmly by the hand, knocked back his drink, and turned and strolled off, through the batwing doors and out of the saloon.

Stone watched him go. He guessed that Brad Gourlay would make his move against the prospector after he had left Mallory and was headed back towards the goldfields. It could prove injudicious to murder O'Brien in town, and Gourlay was not a man to act unwisely. Stone determined, therefore, to rise early the next morning and follow the prospector out of town.

Brad Gourlay, meanwhile, had called at the law office and then, accompanied by Sheriff Joe Banks, had returned to the Ace High Saloon, where he found his brother and Long Tom Russell finishing their breakfast. The four promptly adjourned to the small office next to the bar-counter, and there the mayor addressed the others.

"Wa'al, boys," said Brad Gourlay genially, "reckon we got ourselves another lucky strike."

"The old-timer has struck it rich, has he? There ain't no doubt 'bout that?" rasped Long Tom.

"No doubt whatsoever. O'Brien is obviously an experienced prospector an' he ain't likely to have made no mistake," said Brad Gourlay.

"An' has he registered his claim?" asked Joe Banks.

"Yeah. It was Norman Lowery who brought us news of his arrival in town," said Nathan Gourlay.

"I'm surprised he did that. After the godalmighty scare he got when he was subjected to that investigation, I figured he'd have wanted to play it straight for a while," said Banks.

"You forget how greedy he is," said Brad Gourlay. "He gits well paid for his trouble an' he knows it."

"Guess so. But, why have you included me in this discussion? You don't usually involve me in yore plans," said the sheriff. "'Deed, I thought we'd agreed it was best if I didn't know the exact details, me bein' the law 'n' all?"

"That's right, boss," said Long Tom. "If 'n' you want this old-timer dead, you can leave it to me an' the boys."

"Nope. Not this time, Long Tom," said Brad Gourlay. "As you all know, the Governor has got his eye on us.

In fact, I'm convinced it was him who was behind that recent goddam investigation."

"An investigation that completely cleared our friend, Norman," commented Long Tom.

"Thanks to Nate. But if 'n' the Governor hears that yet another prospector has vanished into thin air, he's liable to wanta take some further action."

"Another investigation?" suggested Nathan Gourlay.

"Yeah, probably. Wa'al, that ain't gonna happen. O'Brien is not about to vanish," said the mayor.

"So, whaddya plan doin', Brad?" asked his brother.

"I ain't gonna do nuthin', an' neither is Long Tom." Brad Gourlay turned to the sheriff. "You, Joe, are gonna gun down O'Brien in the prosecution of yore duty."

"I . . . I don't understand?" said a bewildered Joe Banks.

"I'll explain. It's like this. You swear

in a coupla Long Tom's boys as deppities an' follow O'Brien when he sets off tomorrow mornin' into the hills. You aim to catch up with him somewhere nice 'n' remote, say Cougar Pass for instance. Then you shoot him dead an' bring him back to town. The story is this: O'Brien took his provisions from my store an' then refused to pay. My clerk'll sign an affidavit to that effect. Consequently, you, Joe, in yore capacity as sheriff rode out after the thief an' attempted to arrest him. Unfortunately he pulled a gun on you an', so, you were forced to shoot him. Pure self-defence, an' you got yore two deppities as witnesses to this fact."

"I . . . I don't like this," muttered Joe Banks, for, while the sheriff was happy enough to bend the law at Brad Gourlay's bidding, he preferred to leave the actual acts of murder to Long Tom Russell and his gang.

"I ain't askin' you to like it, Joe," hissed Brad Gourlay. "I'm tellin' you that this is how we do it. This way, we don't give the Governor no excuse to mount any investigation. What is there to investigate, for Pete's sake? Everythin' is out in the open, an all straight 'n' above board."

"But how does that git us O'Brien's claim?" enquired Long Tom.

"Simple. Our pal, Norman, does his usual trick an' alters his records to register the old-timer's claim as that of the Mallory Minin' Company. Then he registers another claim in the name of O'Brien. That useless parcel of land out near Bear Creek'll do jest fine."

"So, if anyone does check up, they'll find that O'Brien has indeed registered his claim!" exclaimed Long Tom.

"Exactly," said the mayor. "Only it'll be worthless."

"Jeeze, that's jest perfect!" cried his brother delightedly.

"Yeah. Seems to be foolproof. You sure have thought of everythin'," said Long Tom.

"I reckon so." Brad Gourlay glanced

towards the sheriff. "You ain't gonna let us down, are you, Joe?" he asked, in a voice charged with menace.

Joe Banks looked less than happy. He knew that he had no choice other than to do as the mayor wanted.

"No, I ain't gonna let you down," he replied sourly.

"Fine!" Brad Gourlay grinned and clapped the lawman on the shoulder. "Let's go git ourselves a drink," he said.

"Yeah. I sure could use one," muttered Joe Banks, whereupon they all trooped out of the office and joined Nancy Carson at the bar of the Ace High. And, straight away, Brad Gourlay ordered drinks all round.

Nancy Carson, for her part, was in no happier frame of mind than the sheriff. She had long loved Brad Gourlay and had even entertained hopes that one day he might marry her. Now those hopes were dashed, for Brad had abandoned her for a nubile young redhead, who had recently arrived at Al Cooney's Jack of Diamonds Saloon. And, worse still, Brad had bequeathed her to his brother, Nathan. It wasn't simply that Nancy didn't love Nathan. The fact was, the man was a sadist, who invariably took great delight in inflicting pain upon the blonde during the course of their lovemaking. As a result, Nancy did not merely dislike him. She hated him. But, like Joe Banks, she dared not cross the mayor. In consequence, she tolerated his brother, though she was never better pleased than when, on the odd occasion, Nathan chose to spend the night with one of her girls. Now, however, she fixed a wide grin to her lips and addressed the four conspirators.

"Wa'al, boys, how's it goin'?" she asked.

"Pretty good," replied Brad Gourlay. "By this time tomorrow, I reckon we'll be a whole heap richer than we are now."

"Is that so? An' how d'you propose to manage that?" said Nancy.

"We're gonna acquire us some land. Some land that's plumb full o' gold." Brad Gourlay tapped his nose and continued silkily, "All we have to do is extract it. Not too difficult a task, I reckon."

"I sure gotta hand it to you, Brad; you don't miss a trick," remarked the blonde.

"Yeah. Wa'al, you gotta play yore part. There's an old-timer, name of Wally O'Brien, who's aimin' to drop in here later, lookin' for a good time. Jest you make sure that he gits it, an' don't try 'n' fleece him."

"No?"

"Nope." Brad Gourlay smiled grimly and added, "Y'see, we want the old feller to enjoy his last night on earth."

5

THE grey skies had given way to blue and the air was fresh and crisp, with a distinct autumnal nip to it. Jack Stone rose early that morning and walked over to the livery stables. He settled up with the hostler and saddled his bay gelding. Then he rode along Main Street as far as Ma Clayton's Eating House. He hitched the gelding to the rail outside the establishment, went inside and ordered breakfast.

The Kentuckian ate his meal at a table next to the window. From this vantage point, he watched Wally O'Brien emerge from the Ace High Saloon and climb wearily into the saddle. He continued to watch as the elderly prospector, leading his mule at a steady trot, rode off down Main Street towards Brad Gourlay's general store.

101

It took Wally O'Brien only a few minutes to purchase his provisions and load them onto the mule. Then, once he was satisfied that everything was secure, he re-mounted his ancient grey mare and headed for the hills. He had scarcely passed beyond the town limits when Sheriff Joe Banks and two of Long Tom Russell's gunslingers stepped out of the law office. They immediately mounted their horses and set off after the old-timer. However, they made no effort to overtake him. Instead, the trio took care to maintain a good distance between themselves and their quarry.

Stone was not fooled, though. He guessed correctly that the sheriff and his two companions were simply biding their time. But he was a little surprised that Joe Banks was to be involved. He had not reckoned on the sheriff playing a part in Wally O'Brien's disappearance.

The Kentuckian took his time finishing his breakfast, then paid his bill and rode out after the others. He did not stick to the trail, but chose instead to keep to the high ground, from whence he could maintain a discreet watch on his quarry's progress through the hills. Stone soon found himself abreast of the sheriff and his confederates, looking down on them from the rims of the various valleys and gulches through which they passed. And, so intent were the three men upon their pursuit of Wally O'Brien, that they completely failed to observe Stone was tracking them.

It was as Wally O'Brien entered the mouth of Cougar Pass that Sheriff Joe Banks eventually caught up with him and ordered him to halt. The old-timer reined in his mare and pulled up the mule. Then he turned to confront his pursuers, and he did not like what he saw. Fat and toad-like, the sheriff levelled a Colt Peacemaker at him, while his two so-called deputies, a weasel-faced, pockmarked ruffian called Veitch and a tough, bearded

Texan called Reese, sat with their long brown leather coats thrown open and their hands hovering above the butts of their Remingtons.

"Hey, what is this?" demanded O'Brien.

"It's the end of the line," said Banks.

"Whaddya mean?"

Wally O'Brien glanced from one to the other with frightened, anxious eyes. The gunmen coldly returned his gaze.

"I mean I'm gonna kill yuh," said the sheriff.

"But . . . but yo're the law!"

"That's right. An' this is gonna be done all nice 'n' legal."

"Nice 'n' legal? I don't see . . ."

"It's simple. Ned Lawton, the clerk at the general store back in Mallory, has jest signed an affidavit to say that you refused to pay for the provisions he gave yuh."

"But that ain't true. I did pay for these provisions. I swear it!"

"Sure you did. However, that ain't the point. The point is, you've struck it lucky out in the hills an' have staked a claim which I'm told could be worth plenty."

"An' you intend killin' me so that you an' yore pardners can git hold of it?" exclaimed O'Brien.

"Yup."

"But the claim's registered in my name."

"That can be altered. Y'see, I have a friend at the Land Registry office."

"You've thought of everythin', haven't yuh?"

"I reckon so. You will be shot while resistin' arrest. As I said, it'll be done all nice 'n' legal."

"But I don't carry me no hand-gun."

"That don't matter. Who's around to witness the fact?"

"I am, Sheriff."

Joe Banks and the others whirled round, to find themselves staring into the cool blue eyes of the Kentuckian. While Banks and O'Brien had been talking, Stone had dismounted. Then, dodging down through the tumble of rocks and boulders which lined both sides of Cougar Pass, he had swiftly descended from the ridge to the floor of the valley. Now he stood not twenty feet away, and clutched in his right hand was his Frontier Model Colt. Banks noted nervously that the muzzle was aimed directly at his heart.

"You . . . you are that feller I interviewed back in Mallory. You said you was considerin' doin' a li'l prospectin' an' that yore name was Smith!" cried the sheriff.

"Guess I wasn't altogether honest with you," said Stone.

"No?"

"Nope. The name's Stone. Jack Stone."

"Stone! I heard of you," said the weasel-faced Veitch. "As I recall, you helped clean up Abilene. You were a goddam ruthless sonofabitch an' pretty darned fast on the draw."

"Still am," remarked Stone. "You wanta try me?"

At odds of three to one, for they could discount Wally O'Brien, the three gunmen reckoned they could out-gun the Kentuckian. But they were wrong.

Joe Banks hastily diverted his aim from the old-timer to Stone. As he did so, Stone squeezed the trigger of his Frontier Model Colt. He was fast and accurate, and the forty-five calibre shell struck the fat, red-faced sheriff between the eyes and exploded out of the back of his skull in a cloud of blood, brains and splintered bone.

Stone's second shot hit Veitch in the chest and toppled him out of the saddle. And then, before Reese could draw a bead on him, Stone flung himself sideways and disappeared behind one of the many large boulders that littered the bottom of Cougar Pass. Consequently, the Texan's response ricocheted harmlessly off the rock-face. In his fury, Reese loosed off another couple of shots, but they, too, struck the boulder and sped away down the gulch. Swearing profusely, the Texan leapt from his horse and made for the cover of a nearby overhang of rock. As he ran, Reese blazed away, hoping to keep Stone pinned down until he had reached the safety of the overhang. But in this he was unsuccessful.

Stone had scrambled along through the screen of rocks and now rose from a point twenty or so feet away from the boulder at which Reese was firing. The Kentuckian took careful aim and again squeezed the trigger of his Frontier Model Colt. It barked twice and two bullets ripped into the Texan in quick succession. One smashed through his rib-cage and exploded inside his chest, while the other blasted a great hole in his throat, puncturing an artery. Reese opened his mouth to scream, but no scream came. A fountain of blood spurted forth and he was dead before he hit the ground.

Veitch, meantime, had struggled to his feet. He was clutching his chest and attempting unsuccessfully to stem the blood which was seeping through his shirt and vest.

"You . . . you bastard!" he screeched. "You . . . you've done for me!"

Raising his Remington, Veitch fired at the Kentuckian. But his hand was shaking and he missed. Stone returned fire. And he did not miss. His fifth shot once again struck the gunslinger in the chest, this time penetrating his black heart and killing him instantly.

The entire shoot-out had lasted only a few seconds and, in that brief passage of time, Jack Stone had killed all three gunmen. The Kentuckian grinned at the old-timer, who, throughout the gun-fight, had sat motionless and white-faced upon his grey mare.

"Don't reckon these fellers'll bother you no more," drawled Stone.

"Don't reckon they will," said Wally O'Brien, a relieved smile splitting his ancient features.

"Nope. That was sure some impressive shootin', Mr Stone," said a voice from behind the Kentuckian.

Stone, who had been in the process of re-loading his revolver, whirled round in surprise. He found himself staring up at a tall, angular figure on horseback. The stranger was dressed in a black frock-coat and stove-pipe hat, and was sitting astride a coal-black stallion. His face was gaunt and lantern-jawed, the mouth severe and his entire aspect decidedly funereal. His cool, grey eyes, however, glinted with humour and, when he smiled, he appeared somewhat less forbidding.

"Who in tarnation are you, an' whaddya think yo're doin', creepin' up on us like that?" demanded Stone.

The stranger politely raised his hat.

"The name's Oliver Nunn, an' I am headin' for Castle Rock, where I got me a trial to conduct. Y'see, I'm circuit judge for the whole of this here territory. An' I certainly wasn't creepin' up on you. Jest passin' this way. Guess you didn't hear me approachin' 'cause you were kinda preoccupied." Judge Nunn nodded

110

towards the three corpses. "Mind you, I figure those fellers had it comin' to them."

"You . . . you heard what was said?" croaked Wally O'Brien. "You heard that crooked sheriff threaten to kill me so as he could jump my claim?"

"So as his boss could jump yore claim," Stone corrected the prospector.

"His boss?"

"Yeah. Brad Gourlay, mayor of Mallory. I reckon he was behind the attempt on yore life."

"You can prove that, can you?" enquired Judge Nunn.

"Nope. But that's why I'm here. I rode to Mallory on Governor Bill Watson's orders, as an undercover investigator."

"Wa'al, I'm sure glad you did, Mr Stone!" declared Wally O'Brien warmly, and he clambered down off his grey mare and offered the Kentuckian his hand. "You sure as hell saved my skin, so anythin' I can do for you, jest you say the word. I'm tellin' yuh, Wally

111

O'Brien's yore friend for life!"

The two men shook hands, watched by Judge Oliver Nunn. At the same time, he carefully reviewed the situation.

"If 'n' the Governor has taken the trouble to send you to investigate the goin's-on in Mallory, I figure things there must be pretty bad," he mused.

"They are," stated Stone. "Brad Gourlay runs Mallory with the help of a bunch of murderin', no-account gunslingers. It's believed he has terrorised all of the original inhabitants an' extorts money from most of 'em. It's also believed he has had his sidekicks murder a number of gold prospectors an' re-register their claims in the name of his minin' company. An audit of the records at Mallory's Land Registry office failed to turn up anythin', but, shortly afterwards, the auditor died in suspicious circumstances. So, y'see, I got me one helluva assignment."

"Hmm. Yes, I do see," said the judge. Then he added quietly, "'Course, Mallory's gonna need a new sheriff, seein' as how you've shot dead its present one."

"Yeah. But me riddin' Mallory of that crooked sonofabitch, Joe Banks, ain't gonna help it's honest citizens none," said Stone.

"No?"

"Nope. Brad Gourlay is sure to rig the next election, to ensure his candidate wins the vote."

"Nevertheless, let's s'pose you was installed as sheriff of Mallory. Would that help you some?"

"Sure would. Findin' evidence agin' Brad Gourlay's well nigh impossible. But, if 'n' I was sheriff of Mallory, why, I could start cleanin' up that hell-hole straight away!"

"The Governor wouldn't object to yo're goin' beyond yore brief an' blowin' yore cover?"

"Nope. So long as I bring Brad Gourlay to book an restore law 'n' order to Mallory, Bill Watson will be more 'n happy." The Kentuckian smiled wryly and shrugged his broad shoulders. "But we're kiddin' ourselves, Judge," he said. "There ain't no way I'd win that election."

"Oh, I'm sure we'll find a way," remarked Judge Nunn confidently.

"You reckon?"

"I reckon. So, let's head on into Mallory an' git you installed as sheriff."

"Okay. If you figure you can do that," said Stone.

"What about me? D'you want me to ride along with you?" asked Wally O'Brien. "You may need me as a witness."

"No; my word'll be good enough. An' I heard an' saw everythin' that happened," said the judge.

"Wa'al, if 'n' yo're sure?" rasped the old-timer.

"Yeah. Yo're free to mosey on out into the hills an' start workin' yore claim," drawled Stone.

And so it was settled. Wally O'Brien helped Stone and the judge heave the corpses of Sheriff Joe Banks and his two confederates across the saddles of

114

their horses. Then, once they had been secured, he remounted his grey mare and, leading the mule, continued on his journey through Cougar Pass. The Kentuckian fetched his horse down from the ridge, and he and Judge Nunn headed back towards Mallory, with the three bushwhackers' horses and their gruesome burdens strung out behind them.

* * *

The arrival in Mallory of Jack Stone, Judge Oliver Nunn and the three corpses caused a minor sensation. As they pulled up in front of the law office, a crowd quickly congregated. It consisted of the majority of Mallory's residents, a fair number of those gamblers, outlaws and other riff-raff who had ridden into town to enjoy what it had to offer, and, of course, the Gourlay brothers and Long Tom Russell and his gang.

In answer to the various questions

thrown at them, Judge Nunn raised a hand and bestowed upon the crowd his most forbidding glare. It took a little while, but, eventually, he succeeded in reducing those gathered round the law office to silence. They waited in anxious anticipation, as he slowly lowered his hand.

"You will naturally want to know how yore sheriff and these other two fellers . . . "

"They were his deppities," snapped Brad Gourlay.

"I see. Wa'al, as I was sayin', you will naturally want to know how they came to git theirselves shot," said the judge.

"We sure do!" cried Long Tom Russell.

"That's right!" yelled Pete Norris, who had been a particular buddy of the Texan, Reese."

"Then, I'll tell you," boomed Judge Nunn, and he proceeded to describe in detail the incident at Cougar Pass.

The crowd listened in silence, but,

when he had finished, there were some ugly mutterings from Long Tom Russell and his men, and Brad Gourlay shouted, "Seems to me Joe Banks was simply doin' his duty an' attemptin' to apprehend a thief."

"Yeah. Whaddya have to say 'bout that?" cried Long Tom.

"You heard what I said," retorted Judge Nunn. "Yore fine, upstandin' sheriff freely admitted that the clerk at the general store was lyin' an' had in fact been paid by Wally O'Brien for the goods taken. Who owns that general store, by the way?" he demanded.

"Er . . . er, I do," admitted Brad Gourlay, a touch uneasily.

"Then, you got some explainin' to do," said the judge.

"Have I indeed? An' jest who are you, an' who's yore gun-happy friend?" snarled the mayor.

"I am Judge Oliver Nunn, the circuit judge in these parts, though, in recent times, I cain't recall bein' asked to administer justice in this here town."

"That's 'cause we're such a law-abidin' community," said Brad Gourlay.

"Or 'cause the law around here is as corrupt as hell," snapped Jack Stone.

"An' jest who are you?"

"Name's Jack Stone. I was appointed by the Governor of this state to investigate the goin's-on in Mallory, an', believe me, that's what I intend to do."

"Oh, yeah? Can you prove that yo're workin' for the Governor? An' can you, Mr Judge, prove who you are?" interposed Nathan Gourlay.

"I dunno 'bout Mr Stone, but that's Judge Nunn," said Larry Cotton, the town's blacksmith. "A coupla years back, I attended a trial in Boulder over which he was presidin'."

"Right. I remember the judge from way back," cried Dick Jones, the sixty-year-old proprietor of Mallory's dry goods store.

"Me, too. I recall him from my days as a shot-gun guard with Wells Fargo," said Seth Bridges, the manager of the stage line depot.

The Gourlay brothers frowned as witness after witness came forward to identify the judge. Brad Gourlay swore beneath his breath and determined to change tack. Joe Banks was dead, and that unfortunately was that. He had no wish, however, that the sheriff's demise should shortly be followed by his arrest.

"Wa'al, folks," he said, forcing a smile, "seems the judge is who he says he is. I guess, therefore, we can take it Mr Stone has indeed been sent here on the Governor's business. But I tell you, gentlemen, we ain't got anythin' to hide. I certainly knew nuthin' 'bout this affair at Cougar Pass. If 'n' Joe Banks was indeed crooked, then he was actin' without my knowledge. Consequently, with his death, the need for any investigation is ended."

"I'll go along with that," said Nathan Gourlay.

"An' me," added Long Tom Russell.

"'Deed, I do declare the mayor is the straightest man I know!"

"Then, all I can say is, you must mix exclusively with hunchbacks an' cripples," yelled the elderly owner of the dry goods store.

Brad Gourlay chose to ignore Dick Jones' remark, though he stored it in his memory. He also ignored the titter of laughter that rippled through the crowd.

"My honour an' honesty ain't the question," he stated. "Joe Banks was elected sheriff by the democratic votes of the good people of Mallory. Seems they made a mistake, but then, that's democracy for you. It ain't perfect. So, we shall jest have to be sure we don't make no mistake next time."

"An' when will that be, Mr Mayor?" enquired Larry Cotton.

"Jest as soon as the arrangements for holdin' an election can be made," Brad Gourlay informed the blacksmith. "But, in the meantime, we shall need someone in charge of law 'n' order.

Therefore, in my capacity as mayor of Mallory, I propose appointin' Long Tom Russell as sheriff up to . . . "

"Oh, no!" cried Judge Nunn.

The judge's exclamation boomed forth, once more reducing the crowd to silence. It was not merely an exclamation. It was also a contradiction, which Nathan Gourlay was quick to challenge.

"Whaddya mean?" he snarled. "My brother is right. We cain't wait till the election. We need a sheriff now, even if he is only a stop-gap."

"I agree," said Judge Nunn.

"Wa'al, then . . . " began Brad Gourlay, but Judge Nunn raised a magisterial hand and stopped him before he could complete what he had to say.

"I don't agree, however, that you should appoint the sheriff," said the judge. "There ain't no legal precedent."

"Then, who . . . ?"

"I shall appoint the man who is to administer law an' order in Mallory for the interregnum."

"Ah! An' jest who have you in mind, Judge?"

"Jack Stone. I appoint Jack Stone sheriff of Mallory."

Brad Gourlay continued to smile, though there was no laughter in his eyes. He had no desire that Stone should pin on the tin star, yet he dared not object.

"Very well," he said. "That's . . . that's okay by me."

"But, Brad . . . " Nathan halted, as he caught his brother's eye.

"I got a clear conscience, an' Mr Stone can certainly rely upon my full co-operation during his term of office," declared the mayor.

"Good! Then, that's settled." Judge Nunn took the sheriff's badge, which he had earlier removed from Joe Banks' cadaver, and pinned it onto Jack Stone's chest. "Okay, Sheriff," he said. "The rest is up to you."

"Thanks, Judge." Stone turned to face the crowd. "From today, folks," he shouted, "law 'n' order will be restored to the streets of Mallory. As of now, anyone who pulls a gun within the town limits, for whatever reason, will be run outta town. An' anyone who bucks my order to leave town is liable to git hisself shot."

Brad Gourlay remained impassive, though inwardly he was fuming with rage. Stone as sheriff was going to be a thorn in his side. Indeed, he was going to be more than that. The mayor determined there and then that Judge Oliver Nunn's interregnum should be an extremely short one.

"Wa'al," he said, "I'll set to an' make arrangements for an election to be held as soon as possible. I'm sure Mr Stone will do his duty, but I feel the sooner we have a democratically elected sheriff the better."

"I quite agree. However, I shall not be happy unless I can personally oversee the election. The unfortunate rumours circulatin' 'bout Mallory, an' the fact that a no-account critter like

Joe Banks got hisself elected last time, make it imperative that the next election for sheriff should be conducted with scrupulous care." Judge Nunn smiled grimly and, turning to Brad Gourlay, asked, "I take it that you will have no objection to my supervisin' the election, Mr Mayor?"

"None," said Brad Gourlay. He smiled to himself. Over the next few days he would use a judicious mixture of threats, cajolery and bribery to persuade the majority of Mallory's citizens to vote for Long Tom Russell. By election day itself, he would have everything sewn up. Let the judge come and observe. His presence would simply serve to validate the election. "It will be a pleasure to have you here, jest to ensure everythin's on the level," he declared.

"Fine. Now, let's see; what's today's date?" said the judge.

"October, twenty-second."

"Hmm. Right. Wa'al, I'm pretty tied up for the next coupla months. 'Deed,

I'm on my way right now to conduct a trial at Castle Rock. So, let's say we hold that there election three months from today. How does January the twenty-second suit you?"

Brad Gourlay's mouth dropped open and he stared wide-eyed at Judge Nunn. He was flabbergasted. He had expected Stone's term of office to last no more than a few days, or maybe a couple of weeks at most.

"Wa'al, folks, is that okay with you?" yelled Stone, in the absence of any response from the mayor.

"Sure is!"

"You bet!"

The cries of approval came thick and fast. Mallory's citizens realised that the appointment of Jack Stone as sheriff could mark the beginning of the end of Brad Gourlay's reign of terror, and they were not about to let the chance slip.

When the mayor eventually recovered his composure, it was too late. The people of Mallory had made their feelings clear. They were more than happy to endorse Stone's term of office.

"D'you reckon three months will be time enough for you to clean up this town?" Judge Nunn quietly asked Stone as they dismounted.

"I reckon," said the Kentuckian.

"Good!" The judge clapped Stone on the shoulder. "Then, let's mosey on over to the stage line depot, an' send a telegraph to yore pal, the Governor, to let him know what's happened," he suggested.

"Yeah. Let's do that."

The two men hitched their horses to the rail in front of the law office and headed across the street towards the depot. And, as the crowd began to disperse, the sombre figure of Bart Brownlee, the town mortician, stepped forward and began to size up the three cadavers. He smiled gloomily at the mayor and said, in deep, sepulchral tones, "Guess you'll be paying the funeral expenses, huh, Mr Mayor?"

Brad Gourlay's reply was short, to the point and undeniably obscene.

6

NONE of the four people, sitting drinking whiskey in the cramped space of the small office, looked particularly happy. Brad Gourlay had a large office at the mayor's house and another, equally large one at the Mallory Mining Company headquarters, but it was in the small office at the Ace High Saloon that he chose to broach those matters which common prudence dictated should be discussed in absolute privacy.

The Gourlay brothers were counting the cost after Jack Stone's first week as sheriff. He had recruited half-a-dozen youngsters, sons of those of Mallory's original inhabitants who were most bitterly opposed to the transformation which Brad Gourlay had wreaked upon their town. With their parents' approval, the youngsters had volunteered to act as deputies. Each morning for one hour, they practised gun-play under Stone's supervision. Then, for the rest of each day and night, they helped him patrol the streets of Mallory. They worked in pairs, each one watching his partner's back and vice-versa. Noisy drunks and brawlers were promptly thrown into jail. Anyone who pulled a gun, whether to settle an argument or simply, out of high spirits, to blast a few shots into the air, was swiftly run out of town. Two men had refused to leave. One Stone had shot dead, the other he had grievously wounded. Both were now beyond the town limits, the first lying in Boot Hill and the second patched up and on a stagecoach bound for Denver. And, as a result of Stone's strict regime, a large number of the riff-raff, who had invaded Mallory, hoping to find a haven untouched by the law, had hastily moved on. Things had already begun to quieten down considerably and the townsfolk were quick to appreciate the change. The Gourlay brothers were not. Brad Gourlay could see his profits declining, and both he and Nathan were worried men.

Long Tom Russell was no happier. While Joe Banks was sheriff, he and his gang had done as they pleased. They had terrorised Mallory's citizens, regularly extracting tribute from the town's storekeepers and also from those homesteaders who lived just outside the town. Only the Bar D and Lazy L ranches had been spared, for Brad Gourlay had thought it would be foolhardy to take on those outfits. The cowboys rode into Mallory every Saturday night with money in their pockets, and they inevitably left with their pockets empty. They were high-spending customers at Brad Gourlay's saloons and bordellos, and he had no wish to lose their goodwill. Besides, he was not convinced that the ranch owners would pay up without a fight. Long Tom had disagreed, but he had nevertheless obeyed Brad Gourlay's instruction to steer clear of the two ranches, and keep his men from picking fights with the cowboys. Everyone else they had quite happily intimidated. And now he was hopping mad. Stone had shot dead two of his men and, so far, Brad Gourlay had forbidden him from exacting revenge.

The fourth person in the room was Nancy Carson. In the past, when she was still Brad Gourlay's woman, she had always been privy to his plans, always included in such discussions, for the mayor respected the blonde's sound common sense. Since he had discarded her for the young redhead at the Jack of Diamonds, however, he had been less inclined to invite her to join him in his deliberations. And Nathan Gourlay had no use for her except in bed, where he continued to treat her with a brutal, unremitting sadism. Therefore, she was as depressed as the others, though for a quite different reason. She still foolishly loved Brad

Gourlay, while she had grown to hate his brother, enduring yet loathing the humiliations inflicted upon her in the privacy of her bedroom. Worst of all, she could see no end to this state of affairs.

"We gotta do somethin', boss. We cain't jest sit back an' do nuthin'," said Long Tom Russell morosely, breaking the silence that enveloped the four.

"Nope. I agree," said Brad Gourlay.

"Then, let me take care of Stone," said Long Tom.

"That won't be so easy, now he's got hisself some deppities," commented Nancy.

"They're only kids, as green as grass," replied Long Tom contemptuously.

"Jest 'cause they're young, don't mean they cain't shoot straight," said Nancy.

"An' they're gittin' more experienced day by day," said Brad Gourlay.

"That's right," agreed the blonde.

Nathan Gourlay stared hard at Nancy and then asked his brother, "What's

Nancy doin' in here? Are you sure it's wise to have a woman like her privy to our secrets?"

"She's got a good brain, Nate; an' she's given me sound advice in the past," said the mayor.

"Wa'al, I don't reckon we need her advice no more. I don't reckon she should be in here with us."

"I'll go if you think . . . " began Nancy.

"No." Brad Gourlay turned to face his younger brother. "I'll decide who does, an' who does not, sit in on these discussions. I know that lately Nancy ain't always been included, but, with things bein' as bad as they are, I figure we need all the help an' advice we can git."

"So, what is yore advice, Nancy?" enquired Nathan.

"I dunno, but certainly I don't think Long Tom should go up agin' Stone. Never mind the deppities. If he an' his boys did succeed in killin' our noo sheriff, then they'd simply give the Governor the excuse he needs to launch a full-scale investigation. An', this time, you wouldn't have some no-account li'l clerk to deal with. No, sirree, you'd find yoreselves facin' a team of US marshals. You mark my word!"

Brad Gourlay nodded glumly. He removed the cigar from between his lips and addressed the others.

"Nancy's right," he said. "We make a move agin' Stone an' we're in big trouble."

"So, what do we do? Let the sonofabitch strut the sidewalks of Mallory like he's cock of the walk?" snarled Long Tom.

"Nope. We gotta figure out some way of gittin' rid of Stone that cain't be laid at our door."

"That's easier said than done," growled Long Tom.

"Yeah. Wa'al, let's give it some thought."

A short period of silence followed Brad Gourlay's suggestion. Then, after a few moments, Nathan Gourlay spoke up.

"S'pose, Brad, that Stone got hisself gunned down by a complete stranger, someone who has no connection with either yoreself or the town of Mallory?" he murmured.

"You got somebody in mind?" asked the mayor.

"No-one in partickler, but I'm sure we could find ourselves some gunslinger who . . . "

"He'd need to be darned good to out-draw that bastard, Stone. Anybody who can take on an' kill Joe Banks, an' Reese, an' Veitch, has gotta be hellish quick an' damned accurate, too."

"Yeah. Wa'al, there are some pretty sharp shooters around. For instance, there's Mad Mickey Pike down in Pueblo," said Nathan.

"Now, he is good!" declared Long Tom enthusiastically.

"But you'd have to contact him somehow or other. How d'you propose doin' that? By telegraph?" asked Nancy.

"Why not? Telegraphs are like the US mail; they're sacrosanct," said Nathan.

"Even so. S'pose Mad Mickey gits careless an' leaves yore message lyin' around?"

"I agree with Nancy," said Brad Gourlay. "We don't wanta chance that kinda evidence gittin' into the wrong hands."

"You got a better idea, then?" rasped his brother.

"Yeah. Reckon I have. It jest, this very minute, came to me," said the mayor.

"Okay. So, whaddya suggest, Brad?"

"I suggest we git that murderin' renegade, Red Lynx, to do our killin' for us."

"Red Lynx!" exclaimed Nancy.

"Yes. He an' his band of redskins are at present rampagin' through the territory murderin' an' rapin' an' pillagin' everywhere they go."

"But why in tarnation should Red Lynx wanta oblige you an' kill Stone?" asked the blonde.

"For guns, an' ammunition, an' whiskey."

"You . . . you'd supply him with guns an ammunition?" Nancy was shocked. She had few morals and fewer scruples, yet she jibbed at the idea of supplying arms to a bloodthirsty savage like Red Lynx. "If 'n' you do, he'll use 'em to kill white folks, includin' innocent women an' children!" she cried.

"So long as he kills Stone, who cares?" snarled Nathan Gourlay.

"I don't like it. It don't seem right. Cain't we figure out some other way to . . ."

"Nope." Brad Gourlay interrupted her. "This is the perfect solution to our problem. I've got it all figured out. This way, Stone gits his deserts an nobody can blame us."

"But . . . but how do you propose contactin' Red Lynx? Hell, the US army are out lookin' for him an' they cain't find him!"

"That's right, Nancy. But the US

army don't have Waco workin' for 'em."

Nancy paused and considered. Waco was a member of Long Tom Russell's gang. Also, he was half white man and half Pawnee Indian.

"You reckon Waco can find Red Lynx?" she murmured.

"Yup. He can send a smoke sigual from the top of Reagan's Peak. If 'n' Red Lynx is anywhere within twenty miles of the Peak, he'll see it."

"He could suspect it of bein' a trap an' refuse to come."

"Mebbe? But I don't think so. Anyways, let's give it a go. Whaddya say, Long Tom?" asked the mayor.

"I reckon Waco could probably fix up a meetin' with that red devil. But what then?" said Long Tom.

"We git Red Lynx an' his Pawnees to hide out in Cougar Pass."

"Where Joe Banks an' the others were killed by Stone?" growled the man in black.

"The very spot. You ain't superstitious,

are yuh, Long Tom?" enquired Brad Gourlay.

"Nope."

"I'm glad 'bout that, for Cougar Pass is one helluva good place to set up an ambush."

"You plannin' to lure Stone out there an' git them redskins to bushwhack him?" said Nathan.

"That's it, Nate."

"But how will you do that?"

"Easy." Brad smiled and drew on his cigar. Then, leaning back in his chair, he said quietly, "There's a homesteader over the other side of Cougar Pass, name of Don Bateman. His homestead is mortgaged to me an', if I was to foreclose, he an' his wife an' three kids would lose everythin'. They'd have no money an' nowhere to go. A goddam awful situation to find yoreself in, you must agree?"

Long Tom grinned, while Nathan merely nodded and Nancy muttered a subdued, "Yes."

"So, I guess Bateman will be only

too happy to do as I tell him. I'll explain that, if 'n' he co-operates, I'll mebbe cancel the mortgage an' make him a present of the deeds of his land. If 'n' he doesn't, however . . . "

"You will foreclose," said the blonde.

"Exactly." Again Brad Gourlay smiled. "It ain't as if I'm gonna ask him to do anythin' much," he said. "All he will have to do, is ride into town an' say he has spotted Red Lynx an' his war-party campin' at the foot of Eagle Rock. Then, once a crowd has gathered, he will offer to lead a posse to the spot, where, with any luck, they'll succeed in takin' the Pawnees by surprise."

"An', naturally, as sheriff, Stone will have no option other than to head that posse. That's goddam brilliant!" exclaimed Nathan Gourlay.

"Yeah. An' I figure he'll take most of them young deppities with him, plus, of course, a number of our more public-spirited citizens." A broad grin split Brad Gourlay's handsome features. "Jest make sure none of yore boys volunteer," he said to Long Tom.

Long Tom's own grin widened.

"You can rely on that, boss," drawled the gunslinger.

"I cain't imagine that Don Bateman is gonna wanta lead Stone an' the others into Red Lynx's ambush," remarked Nancy.

"No?" said the mayor.

"Nope. Hell, once the bullets start flyin' in Cougar Pass, Bateman's as likely to git hit as Stone or anyone else in that posse!"

"Sure he is," agreed Brad Gourlay. "However, I'll tell him that I shall give Red Lynx an' his braves his description an' instruct 'em to make sure 'n' let him ride outta there."

"An' is that really what you'll instruct Red Lynx to do?" asked Nancy.

"'Course not. Waco will tell him to let one or two folks escape, so as they can bring the good news back here to Mallory. This will allow me to immediately send him his arms an' whiskey in a covered wagon, which I can make out is bein' despatched to Cougar Pass to pick up the dead."

"But Waco will also tell him that the homesteader an' our sheriff are on no account to be allowed to escape. Right?" said Nathan.

"That's right, Nate. It's best Bateman gits his, same as Stone."

"You've thought of everythin', haven't you, Brad?" said the blonde.

"I hope so. Once we're rid of Stone, we can start gittin' things back to normal around here. In my capacity as mayor, I shall appoint Long Tom as sheriff for the period up to January the twenty-second, when Judge Nunn is due to return to Mallory. Then, we'll make sure Long Tom is elected fair an' square." Brad Gourlay laughed harshly. "By that time, we'll have Mallory tied up so tight, there won't be a single person prepared to vote agin' him, let alone stand agin' him," he asserted.

Both his brother and Long Tom Russell cheerfully proclaimed that Brad Gourlay's plan seemed absolutely foolproof. Nancy agreed, though she remained unhappy at the thought of their supplying arms to the renegade Pawnee, Red Lynx.

"You want me to git hold of Waco?" asked Long Tom.

"Yeah, an' you ride out with him. I want that deal with Red Lynx set up as soon as possible. Then, once you've persuaded the Injun, I'll mosey on over to Don Bateman's place an' give him his instructions," said the mayor.

"Okay, boss. I'll find Waco an' we'll lam outta here straight away," declared the man in black.

"Fine!" Brad Gourlay rose to his feet. "Wa'al, let's git goin'. I got me some business to attend to, an' you've quite a ride ahead of you, Long Tom."

Of the four who trooped back into the bar-room of the Ace High Saloon, only Nancy had any doubts about the course of action which had been proposed by her one-time lover. While she appreciated the need to eliminate Jack

Stone, the blonde did not like the idea of several of the townsfolk, and most of Stone's deputies, being massacred by Red Lynx and his braves. The deputies were, after all, merely boys. She was in a quandary, for, despite everything, she still carried a torch for Brad Gourlay and was reluctant to betray him.

★ ★ ★

While Brad Gourlay and his fellow-conspirators were planning his demise, the Kentuckian was quietly patrolling the streets of Mallory. Stone had gambled that the mayor would refrain from setting Long Tom Russell and his gang of gunslingers against him and his young deputies. To have done so, would have been to challenge the forces of law and order and give Colorado's Governor an excuse to intervene. And Brad Gourlay was too smart to do that. Consequently, Stone had been afforded a breathing space, during which he could train his deputies and attempt to bring the town of Mallory once more under the rule of law.

The six youngsters, who had been deputised by Stone, were all sons of men from whom Brad Gourlay had been exacting tribute. Sensing that here was a chance to end the mayor's reign of terror, their fathers had agreed to them backing Stone in his crusade against the mayor. They were under no illusions, however, as to the dangers involved, and were naturally anxious for the lives of their sons. The boys, for their part, were heartily sick of the way everyone in town had allowed Brad Gourlay and his desperadoes to ride roughshod over them, and they were only too happy to stand up and be counted. They realised that, if they were to have any kind of future in Mallory, then Brad Gourlay and his kind had to be fought and beaten.

The eldest of the six youngsters was Bob Cotton, a tall, strong, ruddy-cheeked, black-haired nineteen-year-old, the son of the town's blacksmith. Of the remaining five, four were eighteen-year-olds. Tom Bridges, the son of the manager of the stage line depot, was a lanky, tow-haired youth; Harry Jones, son of the dry goods store proprietor, and Nick Cooney, whose father owned the Jack of Diamonds Saloon, were both small, wiry, bright-eyed boys; while Pat Hunney the barber's son, although tubby and slow-moving in other respects, was surprisingly quick on the draw. The sixth deputy was a mere seventeen-year-old named Alec Birch. He was the son of a homesteader who lived on the edge of Mallory, just outside the town limits, and he was a sturdy, rawboned lad.

Stone reflected that he had used his first week in office rather well. The gun-practice had been a great success. All the boys already knew how to handle a gun, but Stone had succeeded in sharpening their reflexes dramatically. He had also laid down a few ground rules. Speed was not all-important, whereas accuracy was essential. Keeping a cool head was also needed. It was better to prevent a gun-fight than initiate one. All of this the Kentuckian had taught his pupils. And, he conceded, they had been eager and willing to learn. So far, during the course of their duties, they had broken up a number of drunken brawls, disarmed some would-be gunfighters, sent belligerents to jail and undesirables packing, and all this without actually firing a single shot. But, sooner or later, they would be forced to fire those revolvers and shotguns which they handled with such skill and assurance. And then what they had gained during their hours of practice would prove vital. It could mean the difference between life and death.

Stone glanced down Main Street. He watched Bob Cotton and Tom Bridges patrolling the north side of the street. Bob carried a shotgun in the crook of his arm, while Tom, being left-handed, wore a Colt Peacemaker on his left thigh. As Stone watched,

146

the two youngsters pushed open the batwing doors of Mooney's Saloon and disappeared inside. Crossing over, further up Main Street, Harry Jones and Nick Cooney headed towards East Street and disappeared past the corner of the stage line depot. They were similarly armed. Of Pat Hunney and Alec Birch there was no sign, but, then, they were minding the law office.

All was peaceful and quiet. Women and children could walk the streets of Mallory without fear of being attacked by some drunk or would-be rapist. With the departure of the vast majority of the riff-raff who had invaded the town, the daylight hours were once again free of tumult and uproar. At night the peace was occasionally broken by some drunken miner or prospector, but there was no malice in them, and a night spent in jail usually served to sober them up.

On Saturday night, the cowboys from the Bar D and Lazy L ranches had ridden into town, keen to spend their hard-earned wages on women and whiskey and gambling. The saloons and the bordellos had enjoyed their usual roaring trade, and there had been a few fights, all of which had ended with the participants cooling off in the cells at the rear of the law office. But there had been no gun-play, nor had any of the cowboys ridden into town firing their guns into the air, as, in times past, had been their custom. The reason for this restraint on their part, was that none of them wanted to be banned from Mallory.

Jack Stone had taken the trouble to ride out to both ranches and explain to the ranchers that anyone pulling a gun within the town limits would be run out of town and forbidden to return. The ranchers, in turn, had informed their hands of this new ordinance. The cowboys had grumbled, but, anxious not to be denied the pleasures on offer in Mallory, had agreed to obey Stone's law. As for the ranchers, they had been secretly rather pleased, for both had lost good men as a result of gunfights in Mallory. Over the previous couple of months alone, two of the Lazy L's cowpokes had been shot dead, while the top hand at the Bar D had been seriously wounded and put out of action for six weeks. Even now, he had still not fully recovered and would, in all likelihood, walk with a limp for the rest of his days.

In consequence, Stone was a popular man not only with the two ranchers, but also with the homesteaders who came into Mallory for provisions, the decent, honest citizens of Mallory and even the rougher element, the prospectors, miners and cowboys, for they were all glad to see the exodus of the outlaws, renegades, card-sharps and pickpockets who had thrived on the town's lawlessness when Joe Banks wore the tin star.

As the Kentuckian slowly approached the Ace High Saloon, Brad and Nathan Gourlay and Long Tom Russell came out. The black-clad gunslinger glanced at Stone and spat contemptuously into the street, his gaze insolent and challenging. Stone ignored him and addressed Brad Gourlay.

"Good morning, Mr Mayor," he drawled. "The weather seems to have taken a turn for the better these last few days." Stone peered up into the calm, blue October sky. "Like the town itself. Kinda quiet an' peaceful," he added pointedly.

"For the moment," growled Brad Gourlay.

"Yeah, Sheriff. This time of year, who knows? There could be squalls a-comin'," said Nathan.

Thereupon, the two Gourlay brothers turned on their heel and headed along the sidewalk towards the Mallory Mining Company offices. Stone watched them vanish inside, then reverted his gaze to the gunslinger, Long Tom Russell.

"Any time you fancy yore chances, jest make yore play," said Stone, pushing back his buckskin jacket so that he could easily reach and draw

150

his Frontier Model Colt.

"Mebbe, one day, I'll do that," responded Long Tom and then, once again spitting into the street, he crossed the dusty thoroughfare and entered the bordello on the opposite side of Main Street.

Stone smiled grimly. He wondered what mischief the three men had been plotting together. A chance glance caught Nancy Carson peering over the top of the saloon's batwing doors. The blonde opened her mouth as though to say something, then seemed to think better of it. She threw the Kentuckian a nervous grin and promptly vanished from view.

7

THE good weather continued
and Long Tom Russell and the
half-breed, Waco, could see for
miles from the top of Reagan's Peak.
Although the skies remained blue, a
cool breeze had whipped up since the
previous day, and Long Tom wore a
long, black, ankle-length leather coat
over his usual attire, while Waco
was clad entirely in buckskins. The
half-breed was, like the white man,
extremely thin, though he was much
the shorter of the two. His harsh, dark
features were not improved by the livid
white scar that ran down his left cheek,
and his black eyes burned murderously
beneath a fiercely beetling brow. Thick,
black, shoulder-length hair was held in
place by a beaded ribbon. Waco looked,
and was, a dangerous man, with his
Remington revolver, his hunting-knife

and, in his saddleboot, his Colt Hartford revolving rifle.

The two men had spent the best part of an hour carrying brushwood from the forest beneath to the top of the peak. Now, while Waco built a fire, Long Tom relaxed with a cheroot, sitting astride his chestnut gelding and holding Waco's roan by the bridle.

The half-breed worked diligently and soon had a fire built to his satisfaction. He extracted a lucifer from a small packet, which he invariably carried in the pocket of his buckskin jacket, and proceeded to light the fire. Then, using a grey blanket, part of his bed-roll, he began to send out smoke signals. The series of signals invited Red Lynx to a rendezvous on the top of Reagan's Peak. Waco repeated this series of signals time after time, until finally the firewood was so diminished that no more smoke could be produced. By this time, it was late afternoon.

"No response, huh?" said Long Tom sourly.

"No."

"Shall we fetch some more brushwood an' try again?" asked the gunslinger.

"I don't think so. If Red Lynx is anywhere in the territory, he will have seen my signals."

"So whaddya suggest we do?"

"We wait. If Red Lynx fails to appear by the time it is dark, then we go."

"Back to Mallory?"

"Yes."

Long Tom Russell nodded. He doubted whether the renegade Pawnee would turn up, but, nevertheless, he resigned himself to wait. And, in the event, the wait proved worthwhile. Exactly one hour after Waco had sent his final signal, a dozen Pawnee braves rode out of the forest and wound their way up the narrow path to the top of Reagan's Peak. Long Tom noted, with some trepidation, that they were armed to the teeth. They carried tomahawks, and stabbing-knives, and a curious mixture of bows and arrows, revolvers and Winchester and Spencer rifles; and,

154

in addition, all of them were wearing war-paint.

Their leader rode a coal-black racing pony. He was a thick-set young fellow, with eagle feathers in his head-dress and bells sewn into his buckskin jacket. Of no more than medium height, he was almost as wide as he was tall. The black war-paint gave his rather broad features a most ferocious appearance, and his eyes glinted fiercely as he viewed the white man and the half-breed. Ominously, he hefted a lethal-looking tomahawk in his right hand.

Waco quickly spoke. The thick-set Indian replied. Long Tom frowned. He had not understood one word, for they had spoken in the Pawnee tongue.

"What are yuh sayin'?" he demanded of the half-breed.

"Jest exchangin' a few courtesies. It is usual with the Pawnees."

"Even with a bloodthirsty savage like Red Lynx? I s'pose this feller is Red Lynx?"

"Yes, he is Red Lynx."

"Wa'al, tell him what Mr Gourlay is offerin'. Hell, he should jump at the chance to replace them bows 'n' arrows with brand-noo Winchesters!"

"Okay."

Waco resumed his talk with the young Indian chief. He carefully explained what Brad Gourlay was offering Red Lynx and his braves. Then he stated what the mayor wanted in return. The gleam in Red Lynx's eyes told him that the Pawnee would be only too happy to massacre Jack Stone and his posse. He smiled inwardly, but then Red Lynx spoke. The renegade wanted more than just the rifles, ammunition and whiskey which Waco had offered.

"Wa'al?" said Long Tom.

"Red Lynx will wait in Cougar Pass an' ambush Stone an' his posse. He promises that neither Stone nor Bateman shall survive," replied Waco.

"Gee, that's great!"

"But he wants more than I have offered him."

"More guns?"

"No. He also wants some white women."

"White women! Why, the dirty . . . !"

"Be careful, Long Tom. Red Lynx may not understand exactly what we are saying, but he can probably guess the gist."

Long Tom blanched. He had no wish to lose his scalp.

"Tell him that we will give him more weapons, or more whiskey, but no women," he suggested.

"No."

"Whaddya mean, no?"

"I am not gonna tell Red Lynx anythin' he does not wish to hear."

Long Tom nodded. He took Waco's point. But he did not like it.

"I dunno if Mr Gourlay will be prepared . . . " he began.

"The boss will do anythin' to get rid of Jack Stone," stated Waco decisively.

Long Tom reflected on this.

"Okay," he said finally. "Tell Red Lynx we agree."

Waco spoke once more to the renegade chief and then listened carefully to Red Lynx's reply, which he relayed to his companion.

"Red Lynx says that first you must supply him as agreed, an' then he will carry out the massacre."

"Oh, no! As soon as news of the massacre reaches Mallory, we will bring a wagon to Cougar Pass. Ostensibly, this'll be to pick up the corpses an' take 'em back to town for a Christian burial. In fact, the wagon will contain the guns, the ammo, the whiskey an' the women," said Long Tom.

Waco turned to Red Lynx and translated the man in black's words. Then, following Red Lynx's response, he asked the gunslinger, "How long will he have to wait?"

"Two or three hours at most," said Long Tom. "He must let one or two of Stone's posse escape so's they can bring news of the massacre to Mallory. Then, once confirmation is received that Stone an' the others are dead,

Mr Gourlay will honour his part of the bargain. Tell Red Lynx that. An' swear on yore mother's grave that we'll play it straight with him."

"An' will we?"

"I reckon so. I don't s'pose Mr Gourlay wants no quarrel with Red Lynx an' his band of savages. Not jest for the sake of a few rifles 'n' crates of whiskey."

"An' white women."

"That demand sure sticks in the gullet. But what the hell? How many women does the sonofabitch want?"

"I shall ask him."

In the event, Red Lynx wanted half a dozen, but, after some further haggling, he finally settled for three. Thereupon, he snapped out a few words of command and two of his braves immediately rode forward and levelled their rifles at the gunslinger.

"What the hell's he sayin'?" demanded a thoroughly alarmed Long Tom Russell.

"He says that you are to stay."

"What! But why in tarnation does he want . . . ?"

"You are his guarantee that Mr Gourlay will honour his part of the bargain."

"Oh, Jeeze!"

Long Tom had spoken glibly when he said that Brad Gourlay would want no quarrel with the Pawnee and, so, would play it straight. But now he was not quite so sure. Certainly, Brad Gourlay would not want to lose him, had indeed planned to make him the next sheriff of Mallory. Even so, Long Tom knew that he was by no means indispensable. As he watched Waco ride off down the mountain path, he prayed that the mayor would indeed honour his part of the bargain.

★ ★ ★

It was dark when Waco rode into Mallory. He hitched the roan to the rail in front of the Ace High Saloon, hurried up the steps onto the stoop and dashed in through the batwing doors. On asking the bartender where he might find Brad Gourlay, the half-breed was informed that the mayor had not been in the Ace High since before noon, but that his brother Nathan was upstairs with Nancy.

Waco did not hesitate. He bounded up the wooden stairway to the upper floor and hurriedly made his way along the walkway to Nancy's bedroom. Then he promptly beat upon the door.

When Nathan Gourlay angrily pulled open the door, it was evident he had only that moment leapt out of bed, for he was naked apart from a pair of trousers hastily thrown on and, as yet, unbuttoned. Nancy, for her part, remained in bed, and she did not succeed in pulling up the sheets until after Waco was afforded a tantalising glimpse of her large, ripe breasts. Nevertheless, she was grateful for Waco's interruption. Sex with a sadist like Nathan Gourlay was an experience she would do almost anything to avoid.

"Wa'al," growled Nathan, "what the hell d'you think yo're doin', bashin' on Nancy's door like that?"

"I have returned from Reagan's Peak," explained Waco.

"I can see that!" Nathan glowered at the half-breed, and then a sudden thought struck him. "Where's Long Tom?" he asked.

"Red Lynx is holding him as a hostage."

"A hostage?"

"Yes. To ensure that yore brother keeps his word and, when Stone an' his posse have been massacred, provides Red Lynx with the guns an' ammunition an' whiskey he has promised."

"I see."

"Long Tom was not happy."

"No, I don't s'pose he was. But he needn't worry. Brad has no intention of double-crossin' Red Lynx."

"I am glad to hear that. For Tom's sake."

"So, why the tearin' hurry?"

"There is somethin' else I thought Mr Gourlay ought to know."

"Oh, yeah?"

"Yes. Red Lynx has made a further demand."

"The greedy bastard! So, what else does the red devil want?"

Waco glanced towards Nancy and shook his head.

"I think I shall tell that to your brother," he said quietly.

Nathan Gourlay had followed the half-breed's glance and immediately understood. And he concurred. He had never approved of Nancy's involvement in his brother's business.

"Okay," he said. "Wait for me downstairs, then we'll mosey on over together to see Brad."

"Where is he to be found?"

"At the Jack of Diamonds. Likely as not in bed with the lovely Lily," replied Nathan, slyly checking to see how Nancy reacted to this mention of the redhead who had displaced her in his brother's affections.

Waco smiled darkly and left the room, closing the door behind him. Straight away, Nathan began to dress, while Nancy rose from the bed and pulled on her dressing-gown. She sat in front of her dressing-table and began to fix her hair. By the time she had finished, Nathan was dressed and ready to go. He smiled sadistically at the blonde.

"Sorry to have to leave you, but don't worry, I'll be back later," he hissed.

Nancy waited until the door had closed, and then threw off her dressing-gown and quickly began to dress. Relief at Nathan Gourlay's departure mingled with her natural curiosity as to what further demand had been made by the renegade Pawnee. Waco had clearly been unwilling to state what it was in front of her. The question was: why was he so reticent? She determined to find out. Throwing a dark blue cape over her low-cut red velvet gown,

Nancy hurried from the room. But she did not descend the stairs into the bar-room. Instead, she ran along the walkway and down the corridor leading to the rear of the Ace High. Then, leaving by a rear door, she slipped down the outside staircase at the back of the saloon.

Keeping to the shadows, Nancy made her way past the rear of the various establishments lining Main Street until, finally, she reached the back of the Jack of Diamonds. She halted in the centre of the yard, where Al Cooney had stacked several crates of whiskey and barrels of beer, some empty and some yet to be sampled by his customers. Upstairs, most of the bedrooms had their curtains drawn, though shafts of yellow light escaped through various chinks. Nancy wondered in which of those bedrooms Brad Gourlay was closeted with the redheaded Lily.

It was fortunate that the back door of the Jack of Diamonds creaked badly, for its creaking served to alert Nancy.

Straight away, she dived out of sight behind a stack of empty beer barrels. From this hiding place, she could observe the three men who stepped out through the lighted doorway. Brad Gourlay, resplendent in his city-style suit and crimson waistcoat, was the first to walk into the yard. He was quickly followed by his brother and the half-breed, Waco. Nathan Gourlay shivered as he stood outside in the chill evening air.

"Hell, Brad!" he complained. "It's darned cold out here! Couldn't we have discussed things inside, in the warm?"

"No, we could not. Secrecy is of the essence, an walls have ears. An', don't forget, Al Cooney's eldest son is one of Stone's deppities."

"Oh, yeah!"

"So, we'll talk over here, where nobody can possibly overhear us."

Nancy Carson smiled. In fact, the three conspirators headed for a spot not six feet away from the barrels

166

behind which she was hiding. From her point of view, they could not have chosen a better place to hold their discussion.

"Okay, Waco," said Nathan. "You said that Red Lynx had made one further demand. So, what else does he want?"

Waco eyed the two brothers closely before replying in a whisper, "He wants three white women."

"An' he's holdin' Long Tom as hostage so as to be sure he gits 'em," added Nathan.

Brad Gourlay swore.

"The red bastard!" he exclaimed.

"Wa'al, whaddya say? Do we supply him with the women?" asked Nathan.

"I . . . I guess so," said the mayor. "Tain't as if we don't have a ready supply. There's one or two at the Ace High who are gittin' a bit long in the tooth. We'd soon need to be replacin' them with younger, prettier gals. Reckon Red Lynx can have them."

"An' jest who have you in mind, Brad?"

"Sally Smith an' Kate Nicholson. Both must be pushin' forty."

"But Red Lynx wants three women. So, who's gonna be the third?"

"Dunno. You got any suggestions, Nate?"

Nathan Gourlay permitted himself a wintry smile.

"Sure have," he said. "Hows about Nancy? She ain't no spring chicken."

Brad Gourlay threw his brother a searching look.

"I thought you an' she . . . " he began.

"Nancy ain't so much fun these days. 'Deed, I was thinkin' of exchangin' her for someone younger, fresher an' rather more accommodatin'," said Nathan.

"Wa'al, Nancy'n' me go back a long ways. An', besides, she manages the Ace High for me, an' does it pretty darned well," said the mayor.

"I reckon I could do that job jest as good," retorted Nathan.

"You?"

"Yeah, why not? You ain't given me no proper job yet."

"No, I ain't, Nate. An' I guess you could do the job," mused Brad Gourlay.

"Also, it'll be easier to explain away the disappearance of Nancy, Sally an' Kate than it would three of the younger girls."

"I s'pose."

"'Course it will, Brad. You can say you considered their whorin' days was jest about over an', so, you set 'em up in, let's say, a dress shop in Denver."

"I ain't that generous, an' folks round here know it."

"If 'n' you declare yo're takin' fifty per cent of the profits, they'll believe you."

"Hmm. Yeah, they might at that. But let's say I set 'em up in a dress shop in "Frisco. Denver's too darned close."

"Okay. An' I'll say I ran 'em over to Colorado Springs in yore rig, so's they could catch the train to 'Frisco," said Nathan.

Brad Gourlay nodded and glanced towards the half-breed.

"Whaddya reckon, Waco?" he asked. "D'you think folks are likely to accept that story?"

"Oh, yes, indeed, Mr Gourlay," stated the breed confidently.

"Good!" Brad Gourlay grinned broadly and pulled three large cigars from the pocket of his crimson velvet vest. He handed one each to his brother and Waco. Then, producing a packet of lucifers, he proceeded to light all three. He took a couple of reflective puffs on his cigar and, thereupon, said quietly, "I guess I'd best head out to Don Bateman's place without delay. That way, I'll git there an' back under cover of darkness, an' Bateman can be in town first thing tomorrow mornin'."

"Which'll mean Stone an' his posse should reach Cougar Pass 'bout noon," commented Nathan.

"That's right. Then all our troubles

will be over," said the mayor, with a chuckle.

The other two laughed harshly and, their secret discussion at an end, the three conspirators turned and went back into the saloon.

Nancy stood stock still behind the stack of empty beer barrels. She was shivering uncontrollably, but not from the chill of the bleak October evening. She was aghast. The love which, despite everything, she had continued to feel for Brad Gourlay, was finally, utterly, dead. It was replaced by a burning hatred and contempt for her erstwhile lover. That he could consider delivering her into the clutches of that savage and bloodthirsty renegade, Red Lynx, was simply appalling.

The blonde wiped away her tears. She knew what she must do. No longer did she owe any loyalty to the mayor and his gang of cut-throats. Quite the contrary.

She proceeded to make her way, by a circuitous route, to the rear of the law office. And, by once again keeping to the shadows, she reached it unobserved. Anxiously, she tapped on the door and waited.

The door was eventually pulled open by young Bob Cotton, the blacksmith's son.

"Why, howdy, Miss Nancy! What can I do for you?" asked the deputy.

"Is there anyone in the cells?" Nancy whispered, quietly ignoring the youngster's question.

"Er . . . no; no, there ain't," replied Bob Cotton.

"That's okay, then," said Nancy and, pushing past him, she hurried inside.

The law office consisted of two sections. The rear quarters comprised a narrow corridor on one side of which stood three cells. A solid wooden door divided this section from the front office, where the sheriff and his deputies were based when not doing their rounds of the town.

"You lookin' to speak to the sheriff?" enquired Bob Cotton.

"Yeah."

"Then, if 'n' you'll come on through to . . ."

Nancy grasped the youngster by the arm and shook her head.

"No," she said. "Nobody must know I'm here, so you jest go fetch Mr Stone."

Bob Cotton stared at her in surprise. He could see that she was pretty upset.

"Okay, ma'am," he said, and he promptly disappeared into the front office, shutting the door behind him.

Nancy waited in the narrow corridor. She continued to shiver and was again close to tears. But she fought to keep a tight control on her emotions. Whatever happened, Brad and Nathan Gourlay must have no idea that she had overheard their evil plan.

Eventually, the door re-opened and the big Kentuckian stepped through into the law office's rear quarters. He carefully closed the door behind him before turning to address the blonde.

"Okay, Miss Nancy, whaddya gotta

173

say for yoreself?" he enquired.

"One helluva lot," said Nancy, and she immediately began to relate the details of Brad Gourlay's murderous scheme.

Stone listened intently, his face grim and his cool blue eyes glinting angrily. Then, when finally Nancy had finished, the Kentuckian swore beneath his breath.

"So, Brad Gourlay is prepared to sacrifice you an' a coupla other gals jest to rid hisself of yours truly," he murmured.

"That's about it," said Nancy.

Stone nodded.

"Let me think," he said, and, rubbing his jaw thoughtfully, he began to formulate a strategy to thwart the mayor's foul plot. It took some minutes, but, eventually, he succeeded in coming up with a plan of campaign, which he was convinced would work perfectly. He smiled at the blonde.

"You figured out a plan?" asked Nancy.

"Yeah. Reckon I have. But I'll need yore co-operation."

"You got it."

"Don't be too quick to agree to my proposal," Stone warned her.

"I'll do anythin' to bring that low-down, connivin' bastard to justice!" declared Nancy fervently.

"All right," said Stone. "Then, jest play along as though you know nuthin'. An', whatever happens, don't panic. I'm gonna kid Brad Gourlay into thinkin' his scheme has worked, so you'll find yoreself bein' taken out to Cougar Pass as planned. But don't worry. You'll be okay."

"You can rely on me, Sheriff. I'll keep my nerve."

"Good! An', afterwards, I'll need you to testify agin' Brad Gourlay, an' his brother, an' Long Tom Russell, an' that crooked li'l Land Registry clerk, Norman Lowery. Will you be prepared to do that, Miss Nancy?" he asked.

"You bet I will," said Nancy.

"Fine!" Stone took the blonde by

the arm and escorted her to the back door of the law office. "Now, don't forget," he said, "you mustn't let Brad Gourlay know that you have overheard his plans."

"Oh, I won't!" promised Nancy, and she swiftly disappeared into the darkness.

Stone closed the door and retraced his steps to the front office, where he was accosted by a curious Bob Cotton.

"What in tarnation did Miss Nancy want?" asked the youngster.

"Miss Nancy didn't want nuthin'. She ain't been here. You didn't see her an' I didn't see her," retorted Stone.

Both Bob Cotton and his fellow-deputy, Tom Bridges, stared in bewilderment at the Kentuckian. Then, all at once, they grasped Stone's meaning.

"Oh, okay!" said Bob Cotton, with a knowing wink.

"Nobody must know that she called here," stated Stone, and, lowering his voice, he went on, "But I'm tellin' you boys, tomorrow we're gonna have ourselves one helluva showdown with Brad Gourlay an' his gang. So, I want you to go fetch the rest of the fellers for a council of war. Oh, an' by the way, who d'you reckon is the best rider among you all?"

"Alec is, I guess," said Tom Bridges.

"An' that black stallion of his is 'bout the best hoss in the whole darned territory!" added Bob Cotton.

"That's good," said Stone, "for he's gonna have a long, hard ride ahead of him tonight."

8

THE weather continued cold but dry when, shortly after first light, Don Bateman galloped into town. He entered Mallory with mixed feelings. A big, square-jawed, ruddy-faced man, Bateman was an honest homesteader who had had a spate of bad luck and, as a result, had had to mortgage his homesteading. A couple of poor harvests meant that he could not afford the repayments and the mortgagee was threatening to foreclose. If he did not do as Brad Gourlay had bidden him, he would lose everything and his wife and family would no longer have a roof over their heads. He felt, therefore, that he had no choice other than to acquiesce to the mayor's wishes. Brad Gourlay's offer to cancel the mortgage and present him with the deeds of his property had clinched the matter. Not that Bateman was either happy with, or proud of, the part he had agreed to play. But he had steeled himself to go through with it, for the sake of his family.

In defiance of Jack Stone's ordinance, the homesteader drew his Remington revolver and loosed off a volley of shots, at the same time pulling up his mare in front of the law office. Immediately, Stone erupted through the law office door and aimed his Frontier Model Colt at the homesteader.

"Put that gun away!" he roared.

Don Bateman quickly dropped the Remington back into its holster.

"Sorry, Sheriff," he cried, "but I was anxious to rouse folks."

Stone observed the citizens of Mallory tumbling out of houses, stores, saloons and bordellos and hurrying towards the law office. Bateman's shots had certainly served their purpose. In no time, a large crowd gathered, and Bateman turned in the saddle to face them.

"Okay," said Stone. "What's this all about?"

"I . . . I've ridden hell for leather to tell you that I spied Red Lynx an' his band of Pawnee renegades campin' jest below Eagle Rock."

"So?" demanded Dick Jones, the elderly dry goods store owner.

"So, I reckon we can mebbe git out there an' capture 'em," said Bateman.

"Capture 'em? You gotta be kiddin'. That's a job for the army," objected Seth Bridges, the manager of the stage line depot.

"Not necessarily. They seemed to me as though they'd been drinkin', an' everyone knows no Injun can hold his liquor. I tell you, we can hit 'em 'fore they even know we're there!" declared Bateman.

"Wa'al, whaddya think, Sheriff?" shouted Pete Norris. He and the rest of Long Tom Russell's gang had been briefed by Brad Gourlay to force Stone into forming a posse.

"Yeah, what's yore opinion?" yelled

a second desperado.

Stone took his time replying. He was not supposed to have had prior warning of Don Bateman's news. Therefore, he pretended to be giving the matter some thought. Eventually, he turned to Don Bateman.

"You reckon them Injuns is drunk?" he said to the homesteader.

"I'm sure of it, Sheriff," replied Bateman.

"So, you figure we can probably take 'em unawares?"

"That's right, Sheriff. You form a posse an' it'll be my pleasure to lead you to where they're camped."

"At the foot of Eagle Rock?"

"Yup."

Stone nodded.

"How many of 'em?" he asked.

"Twelve, includin' Red Lynx."

"Okay. We won't take no chances. I'll leave Alec here in town, to take care of things. The rest of you deppities will come with me. An' I'll want a score of volunteers to ride with us."

"You heard what the sheriff said," cried Bateman. "So, who's comin' along?"

There was no shortage of volunteers. All were incensed by the way Red Lynx and his braves had been rampaging through the territory. To catch the Indians unsuspecting and half-drunk, and to put an end to their depravities, was every man's dream. Consequently, Stone's only problem was in deciding who to exclude from his posse. And, in the general clamour to join the Kentuckian, nobody noticed that none of Long Tom Russell's gang had volunteered.

When, finally, Stone had selected his posse and sworn them in, Brad Gourlay pushed his way to the front of the crowd and, stepping up onto the sidewalk beside the Kentuckian, proceeded to address his fellow-citizens.

"As mayor of Mallory, I would like to say a few words. I am proud, real proud of y'all, an' the way you've responded to this challenge. The death an' destruction of Red Lynx an' his band of bloodthirsty renegades will certainly make Colorado a much safer an' better state in which to live. So, I wish you all God's speed, a famous victory an' a safe return! God bless each an' every one of you!"

Stone noted that the mayor was not offering to ride along, but he made no comment. Instead, he contented himself with saying, "Thank you, Mr Mayor, for those few kind words. An' now, folks, jest as soon as yo're saddled an' ready, we'll be ridin' outta here. So, go to it!"

This was the signal for the crowd to break up, if not to entirely disperse. Those who intended to ride with Stone hurried off to saddle their horses, while the rest remained in small, excited knots, waiting to watch the departure of the posse.

The Gourlay brothers watched with satisfaction from the stoop in front of the Ace High Saloon. As far as they were aware, their plan was working perfectly. Standing beside them, Nancy Carson prayed that Jack Stone knew what he was doing, for, if he did not, then she would end up an Indian's squaw.

The blonde was not the only person who was less than happy at the turn of events. Young Alec Birch had no wish to be left behind, and he told the Kentuckian as much in no uncertain terms.

"Hell, Sheriff!" he cried. "This ain't fair! Why cain't I ride along with you?"

"'Cause somebody's gotta stay in town to keep the peace," retorted Stone.

"But there ain't gonna be no trouble in Mallory."

"We don't know that. 'Sides, yo're plumb tuckered out, Alec."

"No, I ain't."

Stone grinned. The youngster was game. That was for sure. But he had ridden throughout the night and had returned to Mallory only half an hour or so before Don Bateman's arrival in town. Therefore, despite his denial, he had to be pretty darned exhausted.

"You've already done yore bit, Alec," said the Kentuckian.

"But . . ."

"I'm sorry, but I've given you an order an' I expect you to obey it."

Alec Birch glowered, yet he knew in his heart that Stone was right. He sighed and shrugged his shoulders.

"Okay, Sheriff, if that's how it's gotta be," he said quietly.

"Thanks, Alec."

This settled, Stone prepared to leave. He mounted his bay gelding and surveyed his posse. He was satisfied he had chosen the best of Mallory's citizenry, for, in addition to his young deputies, he had such stalwarts as Al Cooney, Larry Cotton, Seth Bridges and Jeff Birch riding along. The last-named had ridden into town that very morning. Intending to pick up some provisions, he had been chatting to his son Alec outside the general store when

Don Bateman galloped up and began shooting. Now he, rather than his son, was to participate in the expedition against Red Lynx.

From his position on the stoop outside the Ace High Saloon, Brad Gourlay raised an arm in salute.

"Good luck, fellers!" cried his brother and, immediately, those citizens of Mallory, who were not included in the posse, began cheering.

Jack Stone raised his grey Stetson and then turned to Don Bateman.

"Okay," he said, "let's lam outta here!"

With the cheers of their fellow-townsfolk ringing in their ears, the posse followed Stone and the homesteader down Main Street and out past the town limits. They galloped along the same trail which the gold prospectors took up into the hills, and Jack Stone reflected that the last time he had ridden this way had been when he went to the aid of Wally O'Brien.

They rode hard and fast, and without stopping, until presently they reached a stand of cottonwoods about a quarter of a mile from Cougar Pass. As they crossed a small clearing in the middle of the wood, Stone suddenly raised a hand and, pulling up his bay gelding, brought the posse to a halt.

"What in tarnation are we stoppin' for, Sheriff?" demanded Don Bateman.

Stone eyed the homesteader coldly.

"You aimin' to take us through Cougar Pass?" he asked.

"Yeah, 'course I am. That's the most direct route to Eagle Rock," replied Bateman.

"Sure it is," said Stone. "Only you know that none of us is gonna make it to Eagle Rock."

"Whaddya mean?" Bateman blanched and sweat suddenly beaded his forehead.

"I mean, Bateman, yo're plannin' to lead us into an ambush. Red Lynx an' his braves are hidin' among the rocks in Cougar Pass, jest waitin' to shoot the hell outta us."

"That . . . that's crazy! Why should Red Lynx . . . ?"

"It's no use, Bateman. I know all about Brad Gourlay's li'l plan," said the Kentuckian, and he went on to tell the rest of the posse what Nancy Carson had told him.

Apart from Stone's young deputies, whom he had already briefed, the others were completely flabbergasted. For some moments they were lost for words. Then, one after another, they began to voice their anger.

"So, to git rid of you, Sheriff, our crooked mayor was willin' to sacrifice all of us!" cried Jeff Birch.

"The sonofabitch!" exclaimed Al Cooney.

"Let's string up this bastard, an' then head back to town an' settle with Brad Gourlay," suggested Seth Bridges.

"No. We'll do this all nice 'n' legal," said Stone. "There will be no lynchin'. Don Bateman's gonna be an excellent witness for the prosecution when Brad Gourlay is brought to trial. In the meantime, we've got that murderin' renegade, Red Lynx, to 'tend to."

"But, Sheriff, if 'n' them redskins is waitin' for us . . . " began a nervous Andy Bentham, a carpenter by trade.

"Don't worry. I've made me a few arrangements, an' it ain't us who are gonna be bushwhacked," said Stone, whereupon he whipped out his Frontier Model Colt and, without warning, rapped Don Bateman hard across the forehead with the barrel of the gun.

The homesteader toppled from his horse and lay motionless on the ground. Immediately, the Kentuckian dismounted, took a length of cord from one of his saddlebags and proceeded to bind Bateman hand and foot. Then, he removed the dark blue kerchief from the unconscious man's neck and gagged him with it. While he dragged Bateman into the shadow of the trees, Tom Bridges led the homesteader's mare into the wood and tethered it to a tree. Thereupon, Jack Stone re-mounted and quietly explained what arrangements he had made regarding Red Lynx and his war-party. When he had finished, nobody, not even the nervous carpenter, was prepared to ride off and miss the opportunity to rid the territory of the Pawnee renegades. All were fired up and ready to go.

"Okay!" yelled Stone. "Let's git goin'!"

The posse approached Cougar Pass at full gallop and then, at the last moment, just as they were about to enter the mouth of the pass, they pulled up their horses, leapt from their saddles and dived into the cover of the nearest rocks. This unexpected manoeuvre had the effect of surprising the Pawnees, causing them to leap up from their various hiding-places on either side of the pass and start firing.

As they did so, a number of blue-coated figures appeared at the top of Cougar Pass and began to pour volley after volley of shots down upon the Indians. At the same time, Stone and his posse opened fire. Caught between two fires, Red Lynx turned angrily to the white man who was crouched down beside him.

"You have tricked us!" cried the young warrior chief, surprising the man in black by speaking in English. Normally, he eschewed the white man's tongue, but, contrary to common belief, he could actually speak it.

"No! No, I swear I . . . " began Long Tom Russell, but the gunslinger never finished what he was going to say.

"Nobody betrays Red Lynx and lives!" screeched the Pawnee, and, pulling a huge, double-edged stabbing-knife from his belt, he plunged it deep into Long Tom's belly.

Long Tom screamed and fell backwards among the rocks. The knife was plunged into his body up to its hilt and had literally skewered the gunslinger, its blade protruding several inches out of his back. He coughed up a huge quantity of blood as he attempted to rise, but failed. His eyes glazed over, his head fell sideways, his long, thin body jerked a couple of times and then he lay quite still.

Red Lynx, meantime, was screaming at the few braves, whom the soldiers on the rim of the pass had not already shot to pieces. He ordered them to mount and ride. And, since the near mouth of Cougar Pass was blocked by Jack Stone and his posse, he yelled at them to ride north, through the pass, in the direction of Eagle Rock. Consequently, the surviving Pawnees scrambled down the steep sides of the pass and hastily mounted their horses, which they had left tethered among the rocks at its bottom. Whooping and hollering, and firing off their rifles, they galloped madly along the trail and straight into the trap set by yet another contingent of blue-coats.

As they rounded the next bend, they were met with a murderous fusillade. All except Red Lynx were unhorsed. He was hit in the chest, but, somehow or other, managed to remain astride his pitch-black racing pony. His eyes gleamed furiously. He screeched defiance at his enemies. A bloodthirsty savage he might be, yet Red Lynx did not lack courage. Clutching his tomahawk in his right hand, he emitted the Pawnee battle-cry and charged pell-mell towards the waiting mass of soldiers.

Bullet after bullet tore into Red Lynx's tough, thick-set body, yet still he kept on coming. Was the Pawnee Chief indestructible, wondered the soldiers, as they continued to blaze away at him? The answer was no. Eventually, just as he reached their front rank, Red Lynx pulled up the pony, raised his tomahawk and, swinging it at the nearest soldier, slowly toppled forward. The tomahawk missed the man by a whisker and its head buried itself in the dusty floor of Cougar Pass. Still clutching its handle, Red Lynx hit the ground and sprawled in the dust, blood seeping out through a dozen or more bullet-holes in his stocky, buckskin-clad frame.

For some moments nobody moved, then the soldiers' commanding officer, a craggy-faced veteran, stepped forward and, with the toe of his boot, gingerly turned over the Pawnee's body. He looked at the Indian chief and smiled grimly. There was no doubt that Red Lynx was dead.

The officer, thereupon, barked out a few commands and, within a few minutes, his entire company of US Cavalry had saddled up behind him. They trotted forward to the mouth of the pass, where they met up with Jack Stone and his posse.

"Captain John Spence, commanding D Company, 12th Regiment US Cavalry, at yore service, Sheriff," said the officer, extending his hand towards the Kentuckian.

The two men shook hands. Both were delighted at the outcome of their joint enterprise. Red Lynx and his band of renegade Pawnees had been completely wiped out. Not one had survived, while only one soldier and two of Stone's posse had been wounded. And of these three wounds, all were flesh wounds and none was in the least serious.

The plan devised by Stone had been a simple one. He had sent Alec Birch to Fort Sheridan, to alert the army to the fact that Red Lynx and his braves were planning an ambush in Cougar Pass. He had suggested that the army despatch a company to the pass, and that they creep up on the Pawnees and then await the arrival of Stone and his posse. By so doing, he had argued, they would between them entirely surround the Indians and, so, succeed in eliminating each and every one of the renegades.

"Wa'al, Cap'n, it seems my plan worked okay," said Stone, with a grin.

"It sure did," replied Captain Spence. "Them pesky Pawnees were so intent upon bushwhackin' you an yore posse, that they never noticed us creepin' up on 'em. Mind you, it was kinda frustratin' waitin' for y'all to arrive. Glad we did, though."

"Yeah."

"Anyways, Sheriff, what are yuh plannin' to do now?"

"I intend trappin' whoever it is Brad Gourlay sends out here with a wagonful of guns an' whiskey an' women for Red Lynx," said Stone.

"But they won't do that now."

"Oh, yes, they will!" Stone turned to Larry Cotton. "Larry," he said, "I want you to ride hell-for-leather back to Mallory an' tell the folk there that, with the single exception of yoreself, the entire posse has been wiped out by Red Lynx an' his braves. That'll be the signal for Brad Gourlay to send out his wagon, on the pretext of bringin' home the dead. An' my guess is, he'll insist on it's bein' escorted by what remains of Long Tom Russell's gang. Talkin' of whom, where is the sonofabitch? He was supposed to be Red Lynx's hostage."

"Is he a tall, thin feller dressed all in black?" enquired a young, fair-haired corporal.

"He is."

"Wa'al, he ain't gonna cause you no more trouble. Guess Red Lynx thought the feller had double-crossed him, for he's run him through with his knife," said the corporal.

"It couldn't have happened to a nicer feller." Stone grinned and then, reverting to the business at hand, asked the blacksmith, "You understand what you gotta do, Larry?"

"Yup."

"You gotta make it convincin' now."

"'Course. But, holy cow, there's gonna be one helluva lot of unhappy folks in Mallory! Leastways, until they discover the truth."

"That cain't be helped. If'n you want Brad Gourlay brought to book, you gotta deceive 'em. You cain't tell nobody the truth, not even yore own wife."

"Okay, Sheriff. I promise I'll do as you say. Hell, I want Mallory to be like it used to be, free from the kinda riff-raff that that connivin', no-account varmint of a mayor has attracted into town!" said the blacksmith.

And, with these words, he mounted his horse and set off, back along the trail towards Mallory.

Stone watched Larry Cotton disappear into the cottonwoods. Then, he ordered Tom Bridges and Pat Hunney to go and fetch Don Bateman and his mare.

"You plannin' another ambush, Sheriff?" said Captain Spence.

"That's right," replied the Kentuckian.

"Could you do with some help?" enquired the cavalry officer.

"Sure could," said Stone thankfully. "I reckon me an' the boys here can handle what's left of the Russell gang, but they are, after all, professional gunslingers. Therefore, some of us might git killed. However, supported by you an' yore men, I figure mebbe we can take 'em without any loss of life, at least on our side."

"Then, you've got our support," declared Captain Spence.

The Kentuckian smiled broadly. He

had high hopes of shortly sending a telegraph to inform his old friend, Governor Bill Watson, that he had finally succeeded in taming the town of Mallory.

9

LARRY COTTON'S gruesome news was greeted with horror by all except the Gourlay brothers. There were wives weeping over the supposed loss of their husbands and mothers doing likewise over their sons. Indeed, the blacksmith's own wife was as upset as any, and it took him all his resolve not to let slip the truth and so relieve her from her suffering. However, he kept his word to Stone and stood by his story.

His announcement had brought the townsfolk once again tumbling out of houses, stores, saloons and bordellos onto Main Street. This time, in the absence of their sheriff, they were looking to their mayor to give them a lead. And Brad Gourlay did not disappoint them.

Resplendent in his dark city-style suit

and crimson vest, he stood outside the Ace High Saloon and addressed the crowd.

"This is dreadful, dreadful news!" he intoned, suppressing his delight and putting on a lugubrious expression. "It is evident that those stinkin' redskins spotted Don Bateman an', guessin' what he was about, set up an ambush for our posse. I don't like to speak ill of the dead, but I fear that Jack Stone, as sheriff an' leader of the posse, must bear some of the blame for this tragedy. I cannot imagine our previous sheriff, the late, lamented Joe Banks, leadin' folks into such a trap. He may have had his faults, yet there's no denyin' he was a pretty shrewd an' perceptive kinda feller."

This sly dig at Jack Stone incited, as Brad Gourlay knew it would, some of the grieving townsfolk to speak out against the Kentuckian. He paused to allow them to give vent to their feelings, and then he continued, "Now, however, is not the time for recriminations. Now is the time for action."

"You . . . you are surely not plannin' to take another posse out after Red Lynx?" cried the barber, Jim Hunney.

"Hell, no!" exclaimed Brad Gourlay. "I'm simply sayin' that someone oughta go bring back the bodies of our dear departed for Christian burial."

"But if 'n' Red Lynx is still lurkin' out there, then . . . " began Dick Jones.

"It's my guess that Red Lynx an his band of murderin' savages will be long gone by now," said the mayor, interrupting the dry goods store proprietor.

"So, who's gonna venture out there?" demanded Larry Cotton.

Brad Gourlay stared into the crowd and caught the eye of Pete Norris, the most senior of Long Tom Russell's henchmen.

"I will, Mr Mayor!" cried the gunslinger, promptly taking his cue.

"Good man!" replied Brad Gourlay.

"An' I will ride with him," said

Waco, who was standing next to Norris.

"Yeah; me an' the boys, we'll go fetch them bodies," stated Pete Norris.

Brad Gourlay nodded.

"Fine! Okay, you'd best come round to the back of the Ace High. I've got a covered wagon there, which you can hitch up an' drive out to Cougar Pass," he said.

This plan was warmly approved by the crowd. All were anxious that the dead should be brought into town, yet none was anxious to ride out to the scene of the supposed massacre. Despite what their mayor had said about Red Lynx being long gone, they were fearful that he and his braves might still be out there somewhere, watching and waiting and keen to slaughter some more white folk. Nobody, therefore, volunteered to join Pete Norris, Waco and the rest of Long Tom Russell's gang on their expedition to Cougar Pass. Which was exactly what Brad Gourlay had been relying upon.

He and Nathan had earlier lured Nancy and the other two saloon girls into the small office next to the bar-counter, where they had been overpowered by Waco and three of his confederates. Then, they had been bound and gagged, and taken and dumped in the covered wagon, alongside the supply of guns, ammunition and whiskey intended for Red Lynx and his band.

A team of four horses was quickly hitched to the wagon. And, with Pete Norris and Waco on the buckboard and the rest of Long Tom's men riding as escort beside it, the wagon rattled off through the alley between the saloon and the Grand Hotel, and into Main Street. A mournful, silent crowd watched its progress out of town and on into the hills, until, eventually, it disappeared round a bend in the trail.

As the townsfolk began to disperse, the Gourlay brothers turned and, pushing their way through the batwing doors, re-entered the Ace High Saloon.

"Guess this calls for a celebratory drink, Nate," said the mayor.

Both men chuckled.

Inside the wagon, however, the three saloon girls were in no mood for celebrating. Far from it. Sally and Kate were sick with fear. Waco had taken great delight in explaining their destiny to them, and both were filled with loathing at the thought of being violated by Red Lynx and his band of savages. They had known many men in their time and had endured some pretty awful experiences, but none, they felt sure, to compare with what was to come. Nancy, on the other hand, held tightly to Jack Stone's promise that no harm would befall her. Nevertheless, she could not help but feel nervous, for there was always a chance that the Kentuckian's plan might have gone wrong.

For the women in the wagon, the ride from Mallory to Cougar Pass seemed to take forever. But, finally, they heard Pete Norris yell "Whoa!" and, a few moments later, the wagon rolled to a halt.

Pete Norris and Waco stared into the mouth of Cougar Pass. It was littered with the prostrate bodies of Jack Stone's posse. Pete Norris laughed.

"Okay, boys, go fetch them corpses!" he yelled.

The others dismounted and strolled nonchalantly towards the mouth of the pass. As they did so, Waco had a sudden worrying thought.

"Where's Red Lynx? An' Long Tom? Why ain't they ridin' out to meet us?" he demanded.

The answer came almost immediately. As the gunslingers approached the prostrate bodies, these suddenly sprang to life and, at the same time, a host of blue-coats rose from behind the rocks on either side of the pass. All levelled either revolvers or rifles at the gunslingers.

"Hands up!" yelled Captain Spence.

Two of the desperadoes attempted to

draw their guns and were promptly shot dead. The rest made no such attempt, but simply raised their hands in the air. Bewildered by the turn of events, they had no fight left in them. They realised that they would be implicated in Brad Gourlay's nefarious scheme and probably end up in jail. But this, they felt, was preferable to being shot to pieces. And they knew there was absolutely no chance of their out-gunning both the posse and Captain Spence's company of blue-coats.

Pete Norris and Waco, however, were made of sterner stuff. They had no inclination to rot in jail if they could help it. Consequently, Waco dived into the wagon and hauled Nancy to her feet. He ripped off her gag and dragged her out onto the buckboard, where she could be seen by everyone. Pulling his hunting-knife from the sheath at his waist, Waco held the blade against the blonde's throat.

"Y'all see this!" yelled Pete Norris,

indicating the half-breed's knife. "You want Waco to slit Miss Nancy's throat, you jest start shootin'.."

"Hell, why not? Let her die!" cried one of the posse.

"Yeah, she's only a goddam whore!" shouted another.

"She's a woman, an' I don't want her killed," retorted Captain Spence. "So, nobody fires unless I give the say-so."

"That's right, Cap'n, you tell 'em!" sneered Norris.

The cavalry officer glared at the two gunmen.

"Okay. Whaddya want?" he asked.

"I want you to let me 'n' Waco ride outta here."

"What about us, Pete?" cried one of the other desperadoes.

"You wouldn't be prepared to let the others go, too, would yuh, Cap'n?" said Norris.

"Nope."

"I didn't think you would. So, here's the deal: you provide us with three hosses an let us ride free, me an' Waco an' Miss Nancy."

"Miss Nancy?"

"Yeah. She comes with us to guarantee our safe passage," said Norris.

"No! No! I . . . !" Nancy began to scream, but her cries were cut short as Waco pressed the razor-sharp blade into her neck, penetrating the skin and drawing blood.

"You shut yore goddam mouth or . . . "

The half-breed's words were drowned by the roar of a forty-five calibre revolver. He threw up his arms, the knife spun from his fingers, and he toppled headfirst off the buckboard, to land spreadeagled between the rear pair of horses. A huge hole decorated the centre of his buckskin jacket, the slug having shattered his spine and lodged in his black heart, killing him instantly.

Pete Norris whirled round, hastily drawing his Remington as he did so. But the gun was barely clear of its holster before the first bullet struck him in the chest. He staggered backwards, and a second shot pierced the middle of his forehead moments before he, too, toppled from the wagon. The gun flew from his hand and Norris landed with a dull thud on top of the lifeless form of the half-breed. There he lay, blood seeping slowly from both his chest wound and the neat hole drilled in his head. His eyes stared sightlessly up into the October sky.

Nancy gasped and glanced round at the Kentuckian, who had clambered into the back of the wagon. In his right hand, Stone held a still smoking Frontier Model Colt. He grinned at the blonde.

"Jeeze, am I glad to see you!" cried Nancy.

"Yeah, wa'al, I figured someone might try holdin' you an' the other girls hostage, so I hid behind them rocks over there. Then, when yore li'l cavalcade came to a halt, I dodged out an' crept up behind you," explained Stone.

"You arrived jest in the nick of time."

"I had to wait till the shootin' was over an' the rest of the gang had surrendered."

"Yeah, I s'pose so. Anyways, Sheriff, I guess you saved my life. Therefore, any time you want a woman for the night, you can have me for free," promised Nancy.

"I might take you up on that, Miss Nancy," replied Stone. "But, for now, let's git you untied."

The next few minutes were spent freeing the three saloon girls and handcuffing the surviving members of Long Tom Russell's gang. When this had been achieved, the desperadoes were unceremoniously dumped in the covered wagon together with Don Bateman, who remained trussed up like a Thanksgiving turkey. Then, Nick Cooney and Harry Jones were detailed by Stone to climb in beside them and shoot anyone who made an attempt to escape.

Thereupon, preparations were made for the posse and the saloon girls to depart.

Jack Stone surveyed the scene with some satisfaction. Brad Gourlay's evil plan had been scotched, Red Lynx and his renegade band had been annihilated, Long Tom Russell's gunslingers were either dead or in handcuffs, and Stone's posse had survived the encounter practically unscathed.

Grinning broadly, the Kentuckian rode over to where Captain John Spence sat astride his black stallion, at the head of his Company of US Cavalry.

"Wa'al, Cap'n," he drawled, "it's been a pleasure workin' with you an' yore men."

"An' with you, Sheriff," replied the veteran cavalryman.

Stone raised his Stetson and Spence saluted. Then the two men parted, and D Company wheeled round and trotted off, back through Cougar Pass in the direction of Fort Sheridan. Stone and his posse, meanwhile, headed south, towards Mallory and a final showdown with the Gourlay brothers.

10

JACK STONE raised his hand and brought the posse to a halt. They were a mile outside town and hidden from it by a bend in the trail. He summoned Bob Cotton, Tom Bridges and Pat Hunney forward. The three youngsters trotted their horses to the head of the small cavalcade and reined in beside the Kentuckian.

"Okay, boys," he said. "Reckon it's time for me to confront Brad Gourlay an' his brother."

"You want us to ride along?" enquired Bob Cotton.

"No," said Stone. "I'm gonna mosey on ahead. Nick an' Harry will remain in the wagon with our prisoners. An' you, Bob, will take command of the posse."

"Right."

"You'll keep 'em here for 'bout ten

minutes, and then head on into town. By that time, I figure I'll have finished what I gotta do."

"You sure you don't want no help?" asked Pat Hunney.

"Nope. Guess I can handle them two brothers. What I want you to do, is escort our prisoners to the law office an' lock 'em up. An' keep Bateman in a separate cell from the others. You can supervise that, Bob, while Pat an' Tom head on over to the Land Registry office an' arrest Norman Lowery."

"An' do we stick him in the same cell as Bateman?" said Bob Cotton.

"That's right. I figure them two will sing like canaries if they think that'll help 'em save their stinkin' necks."

"They'll be star witnesses for the prosecution, huh?" commented Tom Bridges.

"Them an' Nancy."

"You reckon she will testify agin' Brad Gourlay an' his brother?"

"Oh, yes! She ain't ever gonna forgive 'em for plannin' to hand her over to

Red Lynx an' his band of savages."

"Guess not," said Tom Bridges.

"What about the Russell gang? Don't you figure some of them will wanta testify?" asked Bob Cotton.

"Mebbe. Mebbe not." Stone knew what a rough, tough bunch they were. They might have few, if any, scruples, yet such men usually were loyal to their own kind. He doubted, therefore, whether they would be prepared to bear witness against the Gourlay brothers. "Anyways, the three witnesses we've got will be more 'n enough to ensure that, when brought to trial, Brad Gourlay and his brother are convicted," said the Kentuckian.

"Guess they will at that," said Bob Cotton.

"So, you know what you gotta do. An' I'll see y'all in Mallory," said Stone.

"Good luck, Sheriff!" cried the three young deputies in unison.

"Thanks."

Jack Stone grinned and, digging his

heels into the gelding's flanks, he set off along the trail towards Mallory. Behind him, the wagon and its escort waited. Bob Cotton had produced a watch from his vest pocket and was carefully consulting it. He was a young man who believed in obeying orders to the letter, and intended to make sure they did not resume their journey until the ten minutes stipulated by Stone were up.

The Kentuckian, for his part, rode on at a nice, easy pace. He knew that Brad and Nathan Gourlay were not going anywhere. They would be expecting to view his cadaver, and those of the rest of his posse. He chuckled to himself. The cold-blooded, murdering sonsofabitch were going to be in for one helluva shock.

★ ★ ★

The news brought by the blacksmith, Larry Cotton, had stunned Mallory. The townsfolk quietly and sombrely awaited the return of their loved

217

ones for burial. Even the gamblers, prospectors, saloon girls and strangers in town wore a subdued air.

Brad Gourlay's gesture, in sending out a wagon to pick up the dead, had been much appreciated. For the first time in years, the mayor had actually earned the esteem of Mallory's citizens. The irony of this was not lost upon Nathan Gourlay.

"Wa'al, Brad," he drawled, "guess you must be 'bout the most popular man in town. That's some joke, huh?"

"Yeah, that's for sure," grinned the mayor.

The two brothers were standing in the Ace High Saloon, propped against the hammered copper bar-top, drinking whiskies. Apart from Sam the bartender, who was busily polishing glasses at the other end of the bar, and four poker players at a table in one corner of the bar-room, the saloon was deserted. The girls had retired to their rooms, since there was no likelihood of any immediate call upon their services. And those townsfolk, who might normally have been expected to drop in for a late afternoon beer, were at home comforting their wives.

"Let's take our drinks over to that table by the window," suggested Brad Gourlay.

"Okay," said his brother.

The two men strolled slowly across the bar-room and seated themselves at a table, where it was most unlikely they would be overheard either by the bartender or any of the poker players.

"Wa'al, Nate, guess you can now consider yorself as boss of this here saloon, for Nancy won't be comin' back," said the mayor.

"Yeah."

"'Course we shall have to convince folks that Nancy an' the other two left town."

"There ain't no problem. I'll jest explain that I ran 'em over to Colorado Springs to catch their train. That's what we agreed, didn't we?"

"Sure did."

"Wa'al, then!" Nathan Gourlay smiled thinly. "What with the commotion over the massacre at Cougar Pass, I don't reckon nobody will suspect a thing. They'll be kinda preoccupied an' will take my word for it," he declared.

"Not if you never leave town."

"Who's gonna notice whether I do or don't?"

Brad Gourlay glanced towards the bartender, still occupied with polishing his glasses.

"Sam might. Or mebbe one of the other girls."

"I don't think . . . "

"But I do. Therefore, as soon as it's dark, you'd best take my rig an' ride on over to Colorado Springs."

"But that's one helluva ride for nuthin', Brad!"

"It ain't for nuthin'. It's so that, when you return to Mallory, you can say you took them gals with you, an' nobody can contradict you."

"Hmm. Yeah, I s'pose yo're right."

"'Course I am, Nate. You jest make certain you hitch up the rig an' drive it outta town when there's nobody about."

"Seems a lotta trouble to take."

"Exactly." Brad Gourlay wagged a warning finger at his brother. "It's takin' a lotta trouble that's gonna keep us free from any suspicion. An', after recent events, I reckon that's essential. From now on, we play it pretty darned straight. Leastways, we do until that lunkhead of a Governor has forgotten all about us!"

Nathan Gourlay nodded his head in agreement. He could see the logic of his brother's argument and, while he had not the slightest inclination to make the long journey to Colorado Springs and back, he knew that failure to do so could ruin everything.

"Okay," he said. "We do as you say."

"An' we gotta show proper respect for the dead. All Mallory must see that its mayor an' his brother are as shocked as everyone else 'bout the massacre at Cougar Pass."

"'Course. You can rely on me to wear a face as long as a fiddle," promised Nathan, with a sly smile.

"Good!"

The mayor was about to continue when Nathan suddenly frowned and shook his head. Brad Gourlay promptly closed his mouth and glanced up from the table. A wide, approving smile split his features as he watched the redhead, who had replaced Nancy Carson in his affections, enter the saloon and hurry across the bar-room towards them.

Lily Finnegan was fresh, young and beautiful. Although small and petite, she curved in all the right places, and she had by far and away the prettiest face of any saloon girl in Mallory. At twenty years old, the redhead was half Brad Gourlay's age, and he was completely infatuated by her. She was well aware of this fact and was determined that he should remain so. Up to the present, Brad Gourlay had not been the marrying kind, but Lily had plans to change that state of affairs.

"Hi, Brad," she said. "I just heard the news 'bout our posse bein' ambushed by them murderin' redskins."

"Yeah. Terrible, ain't it?" said the mayor.

"You .... you don't think that, havin' shot up the posse, Red Lynx an' his braves will mebbe decide to ride into Mallory an' ....?"

"Not a chance," Brad Gourlay interrupted her. "Ambushin' folks an' makin' hit an' run raids on small, isolated homesteads is all that Red Lynx is capable of doin'. He ain't got enough men to mount an attack on a town the size of Mallory."

"Wa'al, I do hope yo're right, Brad, for the news sure scared me!" declared Lily.

"There ain't no cause for you to fret, my sweet," said Brad Gourlay and, rising to his feet, he placed a comforting arm round the redhead's slender shoulders.

"Mmm. That's nice," she murmured. "I like it when you hold me close. I feel all safe an' secure."

"An' that's how I intend you should feel." Brad Gourlay turned to his brother. "If 'n' you will excuse us, Nate," he said, "I reckon I'll take Lily upstairs. The news of the massacre has evidently upset her, an' I figure she needs some comfortin'."

"Sure. See you both later," replied Nathan, with a grin.

He watched the pair climb the stairs arm in arm and disappear into one of the saloon's many bedrooms. He picked up his whiskey and retraced his steps to the bar. It was his intention to remain there until the return of Pete Norris and his men with the wagonful of corpses. And, while he waited, he determined to run a proprietorial eye over the saloon which he expected shortly to be managing.

Nathan was not left to his own devices for long, though, for some of the townsfolk, who had been anxiously awaiting the return of the wagon, decided to settle their nerves with a little red-eye and, at the same time, warm themselves beside the pot-bellied stove nearest to the bar-counter. However, they were but few in number, and the Ace High Saloon was still nowhere near full when, towards the end of the afternoon, the batwing doors were pushed open and Jack Stone stepped across the threshold.

The big Kentuckian stood just inside the doorway, a tall, menacing figure. His right hand hovered over the butt of his Frontier Model Colt and, once he had engaged the attention of everyone in the saloon, he proceeded slowly, purposefully, towards the bar. Nathan Gourlay paused with his whiskey half-way to his lips, and stared in open-mouthed amazement at the sheriff.

"I . . . I thought Red Lynx an' his redskins had massacred you an the rest of yore posse!" he exclaimed.

"Jest as you an' that no-account

225

brother of yourn planned, huh?" rasped Stone.

"Whaddya mean?"

"You know exactly what I mean. You set up the ambush."

"That . . . that's slander! Me 'n' Brad, we'll sue, if 'n' you don't retract."

"You won't be suin' nobody. Y'see, I got me some prime witnesses, an' I'm gonna make sure you an' the mayor both hang by yore stinkin' necks."

"You reckon?"

Nathan Gourlay's eyes glinted malevolently and he suddenly made a grab for his revolver. But he was no match for the Kentuckian. The Remington had barely cleared leather when the first of Stone's shots struck Nathan in the chest and threw him back against the bar-counter. A second shot hit him in the shoulder and the gun dropped from his nerveless fingers. The colour left his face and he began to slide remorselessly down the side of the bar, until finally he slumped against it in an ungainly sitting position. A huge red stain spread slowly across his chest, soaking his shirt and seeping into his grey velvet vest. Also, there was a smear of blood where he had slid down the side of the counter, for Stone's bullets had ripped clean through the gunslinger's body and erupted out of his back.

The sound of the two shots not only made everyone in the bar-room start; they brought Brad Gourlay dashing out of one of the upstairs bedrooms. The mayor had been in the act of dressing, and was clad in his shirt and trousers and clutching his pearl-handled British Tranter. He took in the scene at one glance, and immediately let out a cry of anguish.

"You you've gone an' shot Nate!" he yelled furiously.

He raised the British Tranter and took aim. And, as he did so, Stone turned and fired. A forty-five calibre slug tore into the mayor's body, hitting him, just as Stone's second shot had hit his brother, in the shoulder. Brad Gourlay screamed, dropped the revolver and reeled backwards.

At that moment, Lily Finnegan appeared out of the bedroom. She gasped at the sight of her wounded lover and, crouching down, quickly scooped up the fallen revolver.

"Drop it!" shouted Stone.

The girl peered anxiously down at the Kentuckian. His Frontier Model Colt was pointing directly at her. She blanched and hastily replaced the gun on the floor of the upper walkway. Then, she slowly rose and pulled her flimsy lace dressing-gown tightly round her otherwise naked body.

"Git back in that bedroom, Miss," snarled Stone.

"Y . . . yessir."

"An' stay there."

Lily needed no second bidding. She darted back into the bedroom and promptly pulled the door shut behind her.

Brad Gourlay, meantime, had slowly

begun to descend the stairs. He clutched his wounded shoulder and spoke through clenched teeth.

"You bastard, Stone!" he hissed. "You'll pay for this! If Nate dies, I'll see to it that . . . "

"He went for his gun. I had no choice but to shoot him. I sure didn't want to, for I was real keen to see him hang, like yo're gonna do."

"Oh, yeah?"

"Yeah. I know all 'bout yore deal with that renegade, Red Lynx. It was me an' my posse that was s'posed to git bushwhacked. Only we turned the tables on the sonofabitch, an' it was him an' his braves who ended up in a trap."

"You cain't prove none of this."

"No?"

"No."

"Then, why, if 'n' you ain't guilty, did you draw on me jest now?"

"'Cause I could see you'd shot Nate."

"That won't do, Mr Mayor. I got

witnesses who will testify agin' you."

Brad Gourlay had by now reached the foot of the stairs and, as Stone attempted to take him by the arm, he angrily pushed the Kentuckian aside and staggered over to where his brother was sitting. He looked down at the fallen gunslinger and attempted a smile.

"How're you doin', Nate?" he asked quietly.

"I . . . I guess I'm dyin', Brad," replied Nathan.

"Nonsense! I'll git Doc Fletcher to patch you up. You'll be as good as new."

"No, Brad. I tell you, I'm dyin'." Nathan peered up at the mayor and muttered, "Things ain't quite worked out the way we planned, have they?"

"I . . . I guess not."

"It's like a feller I once rode with was always sayin'. Scotch Willie, we called him. A strange kinda hombre. The deadliest, meanest sonofabitch I ever did meet, yet forever quotin' poetry.

Would yuh b'lieve it? Anyways, a coupla lines he was fond of spoutin' jest 'bout sum up what's happened to you an' me."

"Yeah?"

"Yeah. They went like this: 'The best-laid schemes o' mice and men Gang aft agley.' Kinda neat, huh?"

Nathan Gourlay had no sooner spoken these words than his eyes glazed over, his jaw dropped open and he toppled sideways, to sprawl motionless in a pool of blood upon the bar-room floor.

"Nate!" cried the mayor, and he made to drop down beside his brother, but Stone grabbed him under the armpit and held him fast.

"He's dead an' there ain't nuthin' you can do for him," said the Kentuckian.

Brad Gourlay stood stock-still for some moments, while he came to terms with the situation in which he found himself. He slowly came to the conclusion that Stone was right. There was nothing he could do for Nathan.

Therefore, he had to look to himself. He rounded on the lawman.

"You said you got witnesses who will testify agin' me. Name them," he snarled.

"Don Bateman. An' Norman Lowery. An' . . . "

"An' me."

The two men turned to see Nancy Carson standing in the doorway, flanked by her fellow saloon girls, Sally Smith and Kate Nicholson.

"You!" exclaimed Brad Gourlay. "Hell, Nancy, we go back a long ways! You wouldn't . . . "

"Oh, yes, I would!" stated the blonde firmly. "Y'see, I overheard you an' Nate an' Waco makin' yore plans last night at the back of the Jack of Diamonds Saloon."

"What!"

"Yo're an evil, coldblooded bastard, Brad. There was a time when I could've forgiven you almost anythin'. 'Deed, I still loved you even after you threw me over for that schemin' li'l redhead,

Lily. But plannin' to massacre all them innocent folks jest to git rid of Stone, an' offerin' Sally, Kate an me to them stinkin' redskins to do with as they liked, that was quite unforgivable." Nancy paused for breath and then added quietly, "I'll see you swing, Brad Gourlay, and afterwards I'll dance on yore grave."

The mayor shot the blonde a look of pure venom, which she returned with interest. Then Stone led him away.

"You gonna git Doc Fletcher over to take a look at my shoulder?" he asked, as they headed across the street towards the law office.

"You bet I am," retorted Stone. "Don't want you dyin' through loss of blood. Not 'fore we hang you."

Two of the law office's three cells were already occupied. The remnants of Long Tom Russell's gang were incarcerated in one, while Don Bateman and Norman Lowery were in the second. Stone locked Brad Gourlay in the third cell and despatched Alec

Birch to fetch the doctor. Then the Kentuckian lit a cheroot and strolled outside.

The previous atmosphere of gloom and despondency had been dispelled, to be replaced with one of relief and rejoicing. The townsfolk were enjoying a double celebration: the safe return of those who had ridden with Stone, and the downfall of Brad Gourlay and his gang. As Stone stepped out onto the stoop, he was immediately confronted by a number of the town's elders, all anxious to congratulate him on the success of his plan. They shook him warmly by the hand and clapped him vigorously on the back, and it was some time before he could get a word in.

"Wa'al, fellers," he said finally, "now it's up to you. Most of you are on the town council an' it'll be yore responsibility to elect the next mayor. So, jest make darned sure you pick someone honest an' decent."

"Don't worry, Sheriff, we've learned our lesson," stated Dick Jones.

"Yeah, an' you can be certain that, from now on, we'll give you all the support we can," added Larry Cotton.

"For as long as I am sheriff' said Stone.

"Whaddya mean?" asked Seth Bridges.

"Wa'al, there's an election due in January," said the Kentuckian.

"I don't reckon there'll be anyone standin' agin' you," declared Larry Cotton. "An', if 'n' there is, hell, you'll win by a landslide!"

"That's for sure!" cried Jim Hunney the barber.

"You are intendin' standin' for office, ain't yuh, Stone?" asked Al Cooney.

"I guess so, for there's still work to be done. Some of the riff-raff encouraged here by Brad Gourlay are still in town, an' will want persuadin' to leave. Strict law enforcement is what Mallory needs, an' that's exactly what I intend givin' it," drawled Stone.

"So, you'll be stayin' around for a while," said Al Cooney.

"Yup."

"Mebbe you'll settle an' . . . "

"No, I don't think so. Sooner or later, I'll git me the urge to move on. I'm a feller with itchy feet, y'see," replied Stone. He smiled at the town elders and, adroitly changing the subject, said, "Anyways, for now, I guess I'll mosey on over to the Ace High, for I sure could sink a few beers!"

So saying, he left them and slowly retraced his steps to the scene of his showdown with the Gourlay brothers.

The Ace High Saloon was packed with celebrating townsfolk, and the crowd round the bar was three to four deep. As Stone pushed his way through the throng towards it, he found his way blocked by a smiling Nancy Carson.

"Can I git you a drink, Sheriff?" she asked. "Or is it somethin' else you came for?" she added seductively.

The Kentuckian grinned.

"I had figured on havin' me a coupla drinks, but I guess they can wait," he said.

"So, are you gonna take me up on

236

that offer I made earlier?" murmured Nancy, her large, ripe breasts heaving excitedly and threatening to escape the confines of her low-cut bodice.

"Yo're goddam right I am," said Stone.

THE END

FARGO: PANAMA GOLD
John Benteen

With foreign money behind him, Buckner was going to destroy the Panama Canal before it could be completed. Fargo's job was to stop Buckner.

FARGO:
THE SHARPSHOOTERS
John Benteen

The Canfield clan, thirty strong were raising hell in Texas. Fargo was tough enough to hold his own against the whole clan.

PISTOL LAW
Paul Evan Lehman

Lance Jones came back to Mustang for just one thing — revenge! Revenge on the people who had him thrown in jail.

FARGO: MASSACRE RIVER
John Benteen

The ambushers up ahead had now blocked the road. Fargo's convoy was a jumble, a perfect target for the insurgents' weapons!

SUNDANCE: DEATH IN THE LAVA
John Benteen

The Modoc's captured the wagon train and its cargo of gold. But now the halfbreed they called Sundance was going after it . . .

HARSH RECKONING
Phil Ketchum

Five years of keeping himself alive in a brutal prison had made Brand tough and careless about who he gunned down . . .

FIGHTING RAMROD
Charles N. Heckelmann

Most men would have cut their losses, but Frazer counted the bullets in his guns and said he'd soak the range in blood before he'd give up another inch of what was his.

LONE GUN
Eric Allen

Smoke Blackbird had been away too long. The Lequires had seized the Blackbird farm, forcing the Indians and settlers off, and no one seemed willing to fight! He had to fight alone.

THE THIRD RIDER
Barry Cord

Mel Rawlins wasn't going to let anything stand in his way. His father was murdered, his two brothers gone. Now Mel rode for vengeance.

McALLISTER ON THE COMANCHE CROSSING
Matt Chisholm

The Comanche, McAllister owes them a life — and the trail is soaked with the blood of the men who had tried to outrun them before.

QUICK-TRIGGER COUNTRY
Clem Colt

Turkey Red hooked up with Curly Bill Graham's outlaw crew. But wholesale murder was out of Turk's line, so when range war flared he bucked the whole border gang alone . . .

CAMPAIGNING
Jim Miller

Ambushed on the Santa Fe trail, Sean Callahan is saved by two Indian strangers. But there'll be more lead and arrows flying before the band join Kit Carson against the Comanches.

BRETT RANDALL, GAMBLER
E. B. Mann

Larry Day had the choice of running away from the law or of assuming a dead man's place. No matter what he decided he was bound to end up dead.

THE GUNSHARP
William R. Cox

The Eggerleys weren't very smart. They trained their sights on Will Carney and Arizona's biggest blood bath began.

THE DEPUTY OF SAN RIANO
Lawrence A. Keating and
Al. P. Nelson

When a man fell dead from his horse, Ed Grant was spotted riding away from the scene. The deputy sheriff rode out after him and came up against everything from gunfire to dynamite.

ARIZONA DRIFTERS
W. C. Tuttle

When drifting Dutton and Lonnie Steelman decide to become partners they find that they have a common enemy in the formidable Thurston brothers.

TOMBSTONE
Matt Braun

Wells Fargo paid Luke Starbuck to outgun the silver-thieving stagecoach gang at Tombstone. Before long Luke can see the only thing bearing fruit in this eldorado will be the gallows tree.

HIGH BORDER RIDERS
Lee Floren

Buckshot McKee and Tortilla Joe cut the trail of a border tough who was running Mexican beef into Texas. They stopped the smuggler in his tracks.

SUNDANCE: SILENT ENEMY
John Benteen

A lone crazed Cheyenne was on a personal war path. They needed to pit one man against one crazed Indian. That man was Sundance.

LASSITER
Jack Slade

Lassiter wasn't the kind of man to listen to reason. Cross him once and he'll hold a grudge for years to come — if he let you live that long.

LAST STAGE TO GOMORRAH
Barry Cord

Jeff Carter, tough ex-riverboat gambler, now had himself a horse ranch that kept him free from gunfights and card games. Until Sturvesant of Wells Fargo showed up.

HEL RIDERS
Ste Mensing

Wade Walk kid brot Juane, was locke in the City jail facin ope at w. Wade was a r ess outlaw, but he was smart, a d he had vowed to have his brother out of jail before morning!

DESERT OF THE DAMNED
Nelson Nye

The law was after him for the murder of a marshal — a murder he didn't commit. Breen was after him for revenge — and Breen wouldn't stop at anything . . . blackmail, a frameup . . . or murder.

DAY OF THE COMANCHEROS
Steven C. Lawrence

Their very name struck terror into men's hearts — the Comancheros, a savage army of cutthroats who swept across Texas, leaving behind a bloodstained trail of robbery and murder.